MW01260182

A revised version of the Scarlet Letter

By: Nathaniel Hawthorne

Modernised and edited by: Jim McGuiggan

Weaver Publications

For Ann Laughlin McGuiggan
Who loves the Lord Jesus
And loved my brother Alex

TABLE OF CONTENTS

1

The Prison Door

A throng of bearded men in sad colored clothes and gray steeplecrowned hats gathered in front of a wooden building that had a heavy oak door studded with iron spikes. There were women there too; some of them bareheaded and others were hooded.

No matter how pious a new colony is and no matter what kind of Utopia they mean to build they must always devote some of their space as a cemetery because they're going to need one by and by. They also understand that they will have to devote some piece of ground for a prison house because they'll need one of those as well.

That being the case we may safely assume that the forefathers of Boston began their cemetery on Isaac Johnson's property around his own grave, which would have become the center of the old churchyard of King's Chapel. What is known to be fact is that some fifteen or twenty years after the settlement of the town the wooden jail they built was weather-stained and marked with age. The age and the stains would only add gloom to the already beetle-browed and gloomy front. With the rust added, the ponderous ironwork on the oak door looked more ancient than anything else in the New World. There they were, the ancient prison ironwork and the New World existing side by side, and like everything else connected with crime the prison and its ironwork seemed never to have been young. In front of this ugly prison house and between it and the wheel-track of the street was a grass plot with burdock, green amaranth and other ugly weeds growing in it. But no weed was as gloomy as the gloomy flower of civilization itself—the prison house. At one side of the door, almost at the entrance, a wild rosebush was growing and since it was June it was in full flower. It might have been offering a final glimpse of beauty and a breath of fragrance before the prisoners heard the door thud behind them and it would be there to say a sympathetic and compassionate goodbye to the condemned prisoners as they were walked to their doom. Some say the rose bush simply survived in the wilderness and continued when other mighty trees that used to tower over it had fallen and others are sure that we owe its existence to the saintly Anne Hutchinson. Whatever; but maybe it's enough that it symbolizes some sweetness and beauty at the door of such a gloomy and hope-killing place and that it will do the same at the beginning of this story of human frailty and sorrow.

2

The Marketplace

A little more than two centuries ago on a summer morning a goodsized crowd of Boston people were gathered on the grassy plot in front of that jail in Prison Lane; their eyes all fixed on the iron clamped oak door. It wouldn't matter where or when this gathering had taken place, one thing was clear from the very look of them— they were there about some profoundly serious business. The execution of some ungodly murderer toward whom the whole colony felt nothing but hatred and bitterness? It could have been, but in those early days and with the severity attached to the Puritan character that would have been too easy an assumption. The truth is, it could as easily have been that a lazy bond-slave or a rebellious child was to be handed over to the civil authorities by frustrated owners or parents to be whipped into submission. It could have been that a member of some sect, an Antinomian or perhaps a Quaker, was to be humiliated and whipped before being thrown out of town. A drunken Indian that had got his hands on too much of the white man's fire-water might need to be beaten back into the forest he came from; he would have generated this kind of interest. It could have been a hanging, like the time they hung old Hibbins, the witch-woman, and bitter-tempered widow of a magistrate. In any case, that was the mood of the crowd of spectators that held law and religion to be nearly the same thing.

What's more, these were the kind of people that thought minor offences were as serious as a major crime. A transgressor had little hope of sympathy from this rigid and in some respects heartless crew. But there was this as well, they saw every act of public punishment, great or small, as a momentous occasion and they invested it with passion and dignity. A public slap on the wrist or a hanging on the gallows was an equally solemn affair. This attitude was the natural outcome of their view that all sin or crime was equally reprehensible.

But on this particular summer morning it was obvious that the women present were especially interested in what was about to happen. These were rough and ready days and the women weren't the genteel creatures we might now think them to be. The rough clothes they wore were matched by their tough moral fiber and nobody thought it strange when big strong women pushed their way through the crowd to get closer to the scaffold at a hanging. The wives and maidens of old English birth were a lot tougher in every way than their smaller, gentler and more refined descendants six or seven generations later. The women around the prison that morning were true descendants of Queen Elizabeth I, that vigorous and masculine representative of their gender. They were her countrywomen, and the beef and ale they swallowed down combined with a moral diet that was no more refined than their food. These weren't dainty, slightly built and timid ladies. They were ruddy in complexion, full-breasted, broad-shouldered and larger women whose speech matched their size in volume and boldness.

"I can't help thinking," said one ugly dame of about fifty, "that it would be a good thing for the colony if we mature women that have good standing in the church were in charge of handling sinners like this Hester Prynne. If this hussy came to be judged before five of us, do you think she'd get away with the light sentence the worshipful magistrates gave her? Bless me, I think not!"

Another one chimed in. "Everybody's saying that the Reverend Master Dimmesdale is cut to the heart that such a scandal should have come on his congregation."

And a third one said, "The magistrates are God-fearing gentlemen but they're definitely too merciful. At the very least they should have branded Hester Prynne's forehead with a hot iron. I'll guarantee she'd have winced at that. The naughty baggage that she is—she'll not care what they put on the bodice of her dress. She could cover it over with a brooch or some heathenish adornment and walk the streets as brazen as ever."

Then a young wife, holding a child by the hand, softly said, "Ah, she can cover the mark however she wants but she'll still have the pang in her heart."

That's when the ugliest and hardest-hearted of this whole self-appointed judge and jury group shouted with obvious frustration, "What are we doing talking about marks and brands on her clothes or forehead? This woman brought shame on all of us and she should be hanged. Isn't that what the law says both in the Scripture and the statute book? If the wives and daughters of the magistrates follow this hussy's example they'll only have themselves to thank."

A man in the crowd burst out. "Mercy on us, missus, is hanging somebody the only way to make other women virtuous? There's no place for that kind of talk. Now you women shut your mouths, they're opening the door, she's coming out!" The door was flung open from the inside and the town beadle came out. Like a dark shadow leaking from the building into the sunshine he came. With a sword by his side and a staff of office in his hand he came. With his gloomy appearance and manner he came, representing, embodying even, the whole dismal and miserable puritanical code of law that it was his job to administer in the strictest interpretation. Aware of the dignity of his position he stretched out the official staff in his left hand and laid his right hand on the shoulder of a young woman just inside the door and drew her forward to the very entrance. At that point the prisoner made it clear that she didn't need or want his assistance and walked out unaided into the open air, asserting her free will. She carried a child in her arms, a baby about three months old. All the baby knew was the twilight and gloom of a room in the prison house so it blinked and squirmed from the blinding light. Then the crowd got a good look at the mother who was holding the baby tightly and close to her breast. Was this motherly instinct or was she trying to hide something that was attached to the front of her dress? If she was trying to hide something that was her shame she must have realized that it made no sense to hide one badge of shame with a baby that was also a mark of her shame. So in a moment she took the baby on her arm and with a faint but defiant smile, although she was blushing, she looked around at the faces in

12

the crowd of her neighbors. She refused to cower. On the front of her dress, in fine red cloth, surrounded with elaborate embroidery and extravagant flourishes of gold thread there was the letter A. It wasn't just an **A**, it was artistic, flamboyant, resplendent—the work of a fertile imagination. It was the kind of rich embroidery they did in the higher circles; no commoner in the colony would be allowed it.

The defiant young woman with the smile was tall, with a figure of perfect elegance fully developed. She had a mass of dark glossy hair, a beautiful face with balanced features, a clean strong brow, a rich complexion and deep dark eyes. She was every inch a lady in the rich way that that word once suggested. She didn't have the surface charm that so easily rubs off as you get older—the thing that substitutes these days for true elegant womanhood. Hester Prynne had never looked more like a real lady than when she stepped out of the door of that prison into a Massachusetts morning. Those who had known her and expected to see a soiled and beaten female creep out of the gloom were astonished at her beauty and her poise. It looked like she had taken her misfortune and shame and woven it into beauty and glory and strength. The very sensitive in the crowd would have seen the threads of pain woven into the radiant picture before them but there was no doubting the radiance.

She had made the dress herself. But she had made it in prison while enduring the shame and the humiliation of being shut off because she wasn't fit company for her neighbors. The dress itself, precisely because she had made it, expressed her feelings, her reckless and defiant mood, and that itself spoke volumes. But it wasn't the dress itself or even the beauty of this woman that

13

mesmerized the startled crowd. It was The Scarlet Letter. Its effect was like a spell. It seemed to add mystery and majesty to the woman and while the spell lasted she wasn't an ordinary person.

"She's a witch with the needle for sure," someone murmured, more to herself than anyone else, and then as if coming out of the spell, "but did ever a woman before this brazen hussy come up with such a way to parade it?" Now into her stride she went on. "All she's doing is mocking our godly magistrates. These good men meant this as a punishment and she's turned it into an exhibition of pride!" Her words went to the heart of the matter. The community meant the letter to be punishment but she was parading it as if she were proud of the stigma. She wasn't only bearing the punishment, she was claiming that she was proud to bear it and that said something about her inner response to what she had done. Could she be repentant about something she was proud of? The hardest looking of the old dames shouted, "I think we'd be doing a good thing if we stripped Madame Hester's rich gown off her dainty shoulders and along with it that red letter with all its fancy stitching. I have a flannel rag we can make one out of, that'd do the job better than the one she has."

"Stop it, neighbors, stop it," their youngest companion hissed, "There's not a stitch in that embroidered letter that isn't stitched into her own heart and she feels every one of them."

The grim beadle, exercising his official position, waved his staff and in a singsong voice, "Make way good people, make way, in the King's name. Open a passage and I promise you that Mistress Prynne will be set where man, woman and child may have a fair sight of her brave garments from this hour until one hour after noon.

14

A blessing on the righteous colony of the Massachusetts, where iniquity is dragged into the sunshine! Come along Madam Hester and show your scarlet letter in the market-place." A lane through the crowd immediately opened and, led by the beadle followed by stern-faced men and harsh glaring women, Hester Prynne walked toward the place of public punishment. Curious schoolboys joined the procession to see what was going on. They didn't really understand what was happening but, then again, what did they care as long as they got some time off school? They ran in front of the procession and stared back at this woman's face, at the baby still troubled by the light and at the letter attached to her dress.

It wasn't far from the prison house to the marketplace but for the prisoner it must have seemed as far as the Tower of London. The procession grew larger with every step as more and more people came to gape. She was outwardly defiant though the parade must have been agony for her since her heart was flung down in the street for everyone to spit and walk on. But doesn't it seem that there's a sort of protection built into us when our souls need to rise to the occasion? Certainly it's true that for some people it's only after the awful experience that they feel the pain most keenly; when looking back on it, remembering, examining and adding details they never thought of at the time. It's then that they invest the jeers and leers with their full quota of malice and cruelty. They were too busy coping with the pain during those awful moments that they had no time to reflect and feel the terrible vexation that comes from doing that.

She reached the place. It was a sort of raised platform at the western end of the market area and almost under the eaves of

Boston's earliest church; at first glance it seemed as if it were a part of the church structure. This raised platform was part of a punishing machine though it has been two or three generations since such a thing has been used. It stands now only as a reminder of the time when people thought it was the perfect instrument for promoting good citizenship—the way the French revolutionaries viewed the guillotine.

On the platform stood the pillory. The pillory! Perfectly suited for the purpose. It's characteristic of those that have behaved shamefully to want to hide their faces from the public's eyes. They walk with their heads down or cover their faces with their hands. They don't want to see or be seen. But the pillory was deliberately designed to hold the head in one place and in one position—face forward. In fact, the face is the only thing really to be seen, certainly the only thing to take the spectator's eye. And isolating the face from the rest of the body forces the entire personality into the face so that the gaping, wondering and perhaps insulting and cruel public can look right down into the shamed soul of the sinner. Modesty is stripped away and there's no hiding. There's no outrage more flagrant and crass against the very person of a sinner than to deprive him of the power to hide his self-shamed face! This is the essence of cruel punishment made glaringly public by this instrument of wood and iron. They aren't used today but there's more than one way to make a public exhibition of a sinner. We only need to keep spreading their shame and they go to work or worship or the market—wherever they go—slyly gaped at, knowing eyes strip away sincerity and call it hypocrisy. "She doesn't know that I know she's the one that [...]. Listen to her, look at her, you'd think

16

butter wouldn't melt in her mouth." Pilloried without the pillory. And since there are always those that hear the story for the first time there is an unending stream of new gawkers. Bravo, courageous pillory-builders, we must keep these sinners before the eyes of the entire populace and it's even more exquisite when they don't know those knowing eyes are weighing them up. Later, when they learn that they've been a spectacle, they'll feel the pain beyond belief. They must be taught that the way of the transgressor is hard and if it doesn't appear to be hard then we must make it hard.

There were exceptions made, of course, and sometimes the sinner wasn't locked into the rack. Hester Prynne, carrying her baby, was one of those exceptions. Knowing what was expected of her, when she reached the place she walked up the steps on to the platform.

And there, shoulder high, the entire crowd was able to look at her, all eyes were able to see her, no one was cheated of his or her privilege to gawk and leer. (And if there were those who might be tempted to violate the laws of the colony here was a good reason to be afraid; a reason to be afraid with a fear that promoted good citizenship.) Had there been a Roman Catholic in the crowd of Puritans he might have thought this beautiful woman was a reminder of the Virgin Mary, the divine illustration of Motherhood. There she was striking in dress and bearing and with the infant in her arms. Of course the beautiful image here would have been a contrast to that sinless motherhood and the baby she bore that was to save the world. These were two mothers and two babies but sin so worked in this case that the world was only uglier in the light of the woman's beauty and more lost in light of the infant she had borne.

There was no humor at the scaffold; they weren't sophisticated enough for that. If it had been her sentence they would have found it easier to watch her hanged than to laugh because their brand of rigid religion hadn't sunk to thinking sin was funny. Besides, there were stern and dignified officials present that made this no occasion for laughter—jeering and mocking were one thing but humor was out of place. There was the Governor himself, and several of his counselors, a judge, a general and the ministers of the town; all of them sitting up in the balcony of the meeting-house looking down on the platform. These people would never risk the loss of reverence of their rank and dignity, so their presence said this was no place for laughing.

A thousand unrelenting eyes burned into her and focused on the scarlet letter on her chest. The unhappy sinner was an impulsive and passionate woman and found the whole situation almost unbearable.

She had prepared herself ahead of time for the insults and public venom but there was something even more terrible about this solemn silence. She could have borne more easily their contorted faces and the roar of laughter and finger pointing. She could have answered all these with a bitter and disdainful smile but this was something else.

Under the leaden weight of this doom she felt like screaming her lungs out and flinging herself on the ground—she felt she was on the verge of madness.

She was saved from the abyss only by the memory of other things that kept coming into her mind and cutting her off from the whole present scene. The crowd and the situation were forgotten, or at least they became mere background as she thought of earlier days. In her mind she was able to leave this place on the edge of the wilderness and go to where other eyes looked at her from under the brims of those steeple-crowned hats. She thought of trivial things from childhood, schooldays, sports, quarrels; she thought of things that happened at home when she was a girl. The images came in swarms but each one, specific and detailed; and mingled with them came the memory of serious and significant events. These she could take pleasure in or at least, these she could control and they held no danger for her. They relieved her to some degree of the terrible weight of the present reality.

She looked back on the path she had been treading since the happy days of her childhood—the road that had led to this miserable place. She saw her hometown in Old England and her old family home, a decayed house of gray stone with the look of poverty written all over it but with a shield of arms above the door. It was worn and hard to read but it bore witness to an old and distinguished family history. She saw her father's face, the bald head and a reverend white beard flowing down over the old-fashioned Elizabethan ruff.

And there was her mother; with her look of attentive but anxious love that was always there. Even after she died that look of love often acted as a gentle protest to some path Hester thought to take and it sometimes kept her from it. She remembered her own face. She used to look into her old dusky mirror and fill it with the glow of

19

her girlish beauty, taking pleasure in how she looked. She could see too another face; the face of an elderly man, pale, thin, scholarly and bleary-eyed from reading many ponderous books by the light of a lamp. But those eyes—they had a strange and penetrating power when the man fixed them on someone, reading their inmost thoughts. He was somewhat hunch-backed.

She thought of narrow and winding streets, tall gray houses, huge cathedrals and ancient massive public buildings of quaint architecture—a Continental city where a new life was waiting for her with the misshapen scholar. A new life, yes, but feeding itself like a tuft of green grass growing on an old crumbling wall. And then, she was back at the coarse marketplace of the Puritan settlement with all the stern townspeople assembled and staring at her. Yes, at her, as she stood on the platform of the pillory, an infant on her arm and the letter **A** in scarlet, fantastically embroidered with gold thread on her chest! Could this be real? She held the child so tightly to her that it let out a cry. She looked down at the scarlet letter, even touched it with her finger to assure herself that the infant and the shame were real. Yes! They were real—everything else had vanished.

3

The Recognition

Being the focus and center of all this sustained and hostile attention was intense but the woman with the scarlet letter saw something that took her mind off the throng and her immediate condition. On the outskirts of the crowd she saw someone that immediately took possession of her thoughts. There were two men; one of them was an Indian dressed in the usual native garb. But Hester had seen Indians before since they frequently visited the town, so that didn't make a prisoner of her mind. No, it was the other man, supported by the Indian that gripped her attention; a white man dressed in a mixture of civilized and savage clothing.

He was small, with a furrowed face that wouldn't exactly be called aged. He looked like an intellectual, like someone whose long mental development had come to show in his outward appearance—you've met people like that. It was clear he was wearing his clothes in an attempt to hide the fact that he was misshapen but she saw that he was hunchbacked. The very instant she saw this thin face and slightly deformed shape she squeezed the baby to her so hard that it cried out in pain, a cry that didn't register with the mother.

As soon as he had come on the scene, and before she had caught sight of him, the stranger had set his eye on Hester Prynne. It was a careless look at first, the look of a man that had seen much and wasn't impressed with much; it was the look of a man that preferred to look within unless he had good reason to do otherwise. The careless look became a keen and penetrating gaze and then a look of horror. It rippled, but quickly, like a snake in continuous motion, only hesitating for a moment before moving on and disappearing from view. His face had darkened with some powerful emotion but he was so controlled that except for that brief passing moment of horror he was the picture of calm. The snake had quickly vanished down into the stranger's deep inner recesses. When he saw the eyes of Hester Prynne fixed on his own and realized that she recognized him he slowly and calmly raised his finger, made a gesture with it in the air and laid it on his lips.

Then touching the townsman next to him on the shoulder he asked him in a formal and courteous manner, "I pray you, good sir, who is this woman? And why is she set up to public shame?"

"You must be a stranger in this region friend," the townsman said, looking curiously at him and his Indian companion, "or you would surely have heard of Mistress Hester Prynne and her evil

22

doings. She has raised a great scandal, I'll tell you that, in godly Master Dimmesdale's church."

"You are right," said the inquirer. "I am a stranger and I've been a wanderer against my will. I have met with grievous ill fortune by sea and land and was taken captive a long time ago by the heathen people to the South. This Indian has brought me here to redeem me out of my slavery. Would you be so good as to tell me of Hester Prynne's—do I have her name right?—of this woman's offences and how exactly she comes to be on that scaffold?"

"Of course, friend. I would think you must be pleased after all your troubles and years in the Wilderness to finally find yourself in our godly New England territory. Here we search out sin and punish it in the sight of rulers and people. That woman yonder, sir, you need to know, was the wife of a certain learned man, English by birth but who had lived a long time in Amsterdam. Quite some time ago he purposed to come here to Massachusetts and join us so he sent his wife ahead of him while he completed some necessary business."

"Bless me, sir, in something like the two years that the woman lived here in Boston she heard nothing from or about Master Prynne. And, as it happened, his young wife left to herself went astray—."

"Ah!—aha!—I understand you," the stranger said with a bitter smile. "In all his learning the learned husband you spoke of should have learned about things like that. And tell me, if you would be so kind, who might be the father of that child she is holding? How old is it, perhaps two or three months?"

"Well, the truth is, the identity of the father is still a riddle waiting for 'a Daniel' to come along and reveal the answer," the informer said.

"Madam Prynne absolutely refuses to speak on that point and the magistrates don't know how to get it out of her. It could be that the guilty partner is somebody standing here watching this, but he's forgetting that God is watching him."

"The learned husband," the stranger said with another smile, "should come himself and look into the mystery."

"Indeed, that would be the answer if he is still alive," the townsman responded. "Our Massachusetts magistracy, taking into account that this woman is young and pretty and no doubt was strongly tempted to her fall, have had the courage and kindness to set aside the full penalty of our righteous law against this sin— death. Bearing that in mind, they have been very merciful, especially since her husband may be at the bottom of the sea. In their tenderness they have doomed Mistress Prynne to stand for three hours on the platform of the pillory and then for the rest of her life to wear a mark of her shame on her bosom."

"A wise sentence!" remarked the stranger, reverently bowing his head. "That way she will be a living sermon against sin until the day when the letter of shame is cut into her tombstone. Still, it disturbs me that her partner in sin should not at least stand by her side on that platform." And then, "But he will be known! He will be known! He will be known!" He bowed courteously to the helpful townsman and whispering a few words to his Indian attendant they made their way through the crowd.

While all this was happening Hester Prynne had been standing on her pedestal, still staring at the stranger. Transfixed! For moments the whole world had vanished and there was no one but Hester and the stranger. The meeting under the present circumstances was horrible while the sun burned down on her shamed face, reflecting on the scarlet badge and with the sin-born infant in her arms. The oppressive crowd was staring at a picture that should only have been seen at a fireside in a happy home or behind a modest veil in a church service. But dreadful as it was, she was conscious of a shelter in the presence of all these witnesses. She knew it was better to stand this way with so many people between him and her rather than to meet him face to face alone. She fled for refuge, as it were, to the public exposure and dreaded the moment when the crowd would no longer be there to protect her. Lost in these thoughts she didn't hear the voice behind her until it had repeated her name more than once in a loud and solemn tone. "Listen to me Hester Prynne," the voice said.

I mentioned earlier that directly above the platform there was a balcony, a kind of open gallery, connected to the meeting-house. It was from there that the assembled magistrates made proclamations on solemn occasions when all the ceremonial niceties were observed. And on this occasion, to witness the scene, was Governor Bellingham himself with four sergeants carrying lances as a guard of honor. He wore a dark feather in his hat, a border of embroidery on his cloak and a black velvet tunic underneath; he was a gentleman advanced in years and with experience written into the many lines on his face. He was suited to be the head and representative of a community that owed its origin and developed

25

state to the stern and balanced energies of mature manhood and the sober wisdom of age rather than the impulse of youth. This stern and sober wisdom and balance accomplished so much because it took no risks and imagined and hoped so little. It was conservative; it aimed to keep rather than to gain. The other eminent characters surrounding the chief ruler were distinguished and carried themselves with that sense of dignity that in earlier years felt that the forms of authority were sacred, divine institutions. No doubt they were good men, just and wise. But out of the whole human family it would have been difficult to choose the same number of wise and virtuous persons less suited to sit in judgement on an erring woman's heart.

This group of sages with their rigid faces that Hester Prynne now looked at was the least equipped to disentangle the mesh of good and evil that came together in this woman's heart. She was clearly conscious that if she were to get any sympathy at all she would get it from the larger and warmer heart of the crowd, because as she lifted her eyes to the balcony and saw these passionless leaders the unhappy woman grew pale and trembled.

She had finally heard the voice of the reverend and famous John Wilson, the oldest clergyman in Boston, and a great scholar like most of his colleagues in the profession. He had a kind and genial spirit but he had suppressed it and developed his intellectual gifts. In fact, in this hard environment, rather than being pleased that he had a kind spirit he was more ashamed. There he stood; a border of gray hair was showing from beneath his skullcap while his gray eyes blinked against the bright light. He looked like one of those darkly engraved portraits that we see in books of old sermons. And he had no more right than one of those portraits had to meddle with a question of human guilt, passion and anguish.

"Hester Prynne," said the clergyman, putting his hand on the shoulder of a pale young man beside him as he spoke, "I have argued with my young brother here, under whose preaching you have been privileged to sit. I have tried hard to persuade this godly young man that he should deal with you, here in the face of Heaven, and before these wise and upright rulers, and in the hearing of all the people, in light of the blackness and the vileness of your sin. Knowing you better than I, he would be a better judge of what arguments to use, whether of tenderness or terror, to overcome your hardness and stubbornness. Perhaps he could persuade you to reveal the name of the man who tempted you to this grievous fall. But he proposes to me (with a young man's over-softness, though with a wisdom beyond his years) that it wrongs the very nature of a woman to force her to lay open her heart's secrets in such broad daylight, and especially in the presence of so great a multitude. It's true that I tried to convince him that the real shame lay in committing the sin rather than in confessing it." And turning to the young minister he asked, "What do you say, Brother Dimmesdale? Must it be you or I that will deal with this poor sinner's soul?" There was a murmur among the dignified and revered occupants of the balcony and Governor Bellingham spoke for them. In an authoritative voice that was balanced with respect for the young clergyman he addressed, he said, "Good Master Dimmesdale the responsibility for this woman's soul lies greatly with you. It rests on you, then, to exhort her to repentance and to confession as a proof and consequence of that repentance."

The plainness and good sense of this appeal drew the eyes of the whole crowd on to the Reverend Mr. Dimmesdale, a young clergyman who had come from one of the great English universities.

He brought with him all the learning of the age into our wild forestland and his eloquence and religious fervor had already shown that he would make his mark in his profession. He was a person of very striking appearance, with an impressive face, large brown and melancholy eyes and a mouth which, unless it was forcibly compressed, was liable to tremble. Clearly he was both nervous and at the same time exercising great self-control. Despite his brilliance, scholarly achievements and natural gifts there was an air about this young minister—an air of apprehension, a startled, half-frightened look; as if he felt he had lost his way on life's path. He acted like an awkward loner that found himself stranded in the public eye. This was the truth about him because, though it never for a moment interfered with his duties in any shape or form, as soon as he was free to do it he withdrew and remained alone. When he needed to he showed himself, simple and childlike and with a freshness and fragrance and purity of thought that greatly affected people. Many of them said his speech was angelic.

That was the young man the Reverend Wilson and the Governor introduced so openly to the notice of the crowd, urging him to speak before them all to that mystery of the woman's soul, so sacred even in its pollution. This desperate setting drove the blood from his cheeks and made his lips tremble.

"Speak to the woman, my brother," said Mr. Wilson. "It is vitally important to her soul and, as the worshipful Governor has said, critical to your own since her soul is in your charge. Exhort her then to confess the truth." The Reverend Mr. Dimmesdale bent his head and appeared to pray in silence and then he stepped forward.

"Hester Prynne," he said, leaning over the balcony and looking earnestly into her eyes, "you hear what this good man says and you see why I am compelled to speak as I do. If you feel it to be for your soul's peace and that by it your earthly punishment will more surely lead to your salvation, I charge you to speak the name of your fellow-sinner and fellow-sufferer! Do not be silent from any mistaken pity and tenderness for him. For, believe me, Hester, even if he were to step down from a high place and stand there beside you in your shame it would be better for him than to hide a guilty heart throughout his life. What can your silence do for him except perhaps to tempt— yes, perhaps compel him—to add hypocrisy to his sin? Heaven has given you an open shame that by it you may work out an open triumph over the inner evil and the outer sorrow. Remember that by your silence you deny to him the bitter but wholesome cup that is now pressed to your lips." The young pastor's voice was sweet and trembling, rich, deep and broken. The depth of his feeling rather than what his words meant to achieve made every heart tremble and the crowd united in sympathy.

Even the baby in Hester's arms was affected by the tone because it lost that vacant look and turned in the direction of the voice and held out its arms to Mr. Dimmesdale with a half-pleased and half-sorrowing murmur. The preacher's appeal was so powerful and had so affected the crowd that they were sure Hester Prynne would speak the guilty name. Or if she made no move, they felt sure the guilty man however prominent or obscure would feel compelled to climb the steps and take his place with Hester on the scaffolding. But she shook her head, signaling that she would not do it.

The Reverend Wilson couldn't remain silent and harshly thundered at her, "Woman, don't transgress beyond the limits of Heaven's mercy! That little baby has been gifted with a voice to second and confirm the counsel you have heard. Speak out the name! Do that and your repentance may lead to the removal of the scarlet letter."

"Never!" she said, not looking at Mr. Wilson but into the deep and troubled eyes of the younger clergyman. "It is too deeply branded. You cannot take it off. And I wish I could endure his agony as well as mine!"

Another voice from the crowd around the scaffold, cold and stern said, "Speak woman! Speak and give your child a father."

"I will not speak!" she answered, turning pale as death because she knew that voice too well. "My child must seek a heavenly Father for I tell you she will never know an earthly one!"

Mr. Dimmesdale had been leaning over the balcony with his hand on his heart, waiting for her response to his appeal. "She will not speak!" he said with a long, drawn-out sigh.

"Wondrous strength and generosity of a woman's heart. She will not speak."

Realizing that they weren't going to change the sinner's mind the elder clergyman, who had prepared himself ahead of time for such a response, preached to the crowd for more than an hour. He discoursed on sin and all its forms but constantly referred to the shame-filled letter on the transgressor's breast. Before he was done the scarlet letter assumed new terrors in their imagination; it was as if its color had got its hue from the red flames of hell itself. All the while Hester Prynne stood there, eyes now glazed and with an air of weary indifference. The entire morning she had endured all that human nature could bear and because she wasn't the kind that would weaken and faint under intense pressure she simply had to shut it all out behind a stony and stoic crust.

In that state the merciless thundering that rolled over her from the preacher made not the slightest impression on her—she was deaf to it. During this time the baby pierced the air with its screams and wailing. She worked at trying to hush it but it was mechanical more than sympathetic. She maintained that same attitude when they finally took her back to prison and she vanished from public view behind the iron-clamped door. In was rumored by those who peered in after her that the scarlet letter threw a lurid gleam along the dark passage that led to her place in there.

4

The Interview

Back in prison Hester Prynne seemed to be on the verge of a nervous breakdown, so the authorities monitored her carefully in case she tried to injure herself or the baby. All day she was wildly rebellious and paid no attention to rebukes or threats and night was approaching. Mr. Brackett, the jailer, brought in a doctor. This doctor, he said, was skilled in all the modern ways of medicine but he was familiar also with the Indian wisdom about medicinal roots and herbs that grew in nature. Bringing in a doctor was a wise move because Hester truly needed help and the baby needed it even more than the mother. It looked as though the baby not only drank the milk from its mother's breast but that with it she was drinking all the chaos and agitation that was in her mother's heart. If the mother

33

was enduring moral and emotional agony of soul the daughter seemed to be expressing it physically because she was screaming in pain and writhing in a series of convulsions.

The jailer, near to distraction, led the doctor in to the dismal room.

The doctor didn't have to come very far because he too was staying in the prison house. He had done no wrong nor was he accused of any. It was simply the most convenient place to house him until the authorities completed his ransom from the Indians. The jailer brought him in and announced him as Roger Chillingworth and as soon as he entered the room Hester Prynne became still as death—he was the misshapen figure in the crowd, her husband Mr. Prynne. The jailer was astonished at the instant effect the visitor had on the woman.

"Please, friend, leave me alone with my patient," the doctor said.

"Trust me good jailer, before long you will have peace and quietness in your own house. And I can promise you that after this Mistress Prynne will not be giving you any further trouble. She will be obedient."

"I don't think so," said Mr. Brackett, "but if your worship can accomplish that I'll call you a miracle worker. I'm telling you the truth, you would think this woman had been possessed and I was on the verge of flailing the Devil out of her with a whip." The visitor had entered the room with that quiet professional air that's usual with doctors, which is what he had claimed to be. And he maintained that calm professionalism when the jailer left him face to face with the woman who had been spellbound by the sight of him when she spotted him in the crowd. His first order of business while Hester watched him in utter silence was to carefully check the baby.

Then from under his garment he took a leather pouch and unclasped it. It was obvious that they were medical preparations and he took one of them and mixed it with a cup of water.

"My old studies in alchemy," he murmured, "and my stay for more than a year with the Indian people who are expert in the healing properties of natural herbs and roots have made a better physician of me than many that claim the medical degree. Here, woman! The child is yours—she is none of mine—and she won't recognize me in any way as a father. So give her this drink with your own hand." Looking hard into his face, Hester had fear written all over her and refused to take the drink.

"Would you avenge yourself on the innocent baby?" she whispered.

"Foolish woman!" the doctor said, soothingly but unable to hide the chill. "Do you think I'm mad? Why would I want to harm this misbegotten and miserable baby? The medicine is powerful and will do it good. If it were my child—yes, mine as well as yours—I could do no better for it." But in her state of mind she couldn't think straight and continued to hesitate, so he took the infant in his arms and gave it the drink.

Before long it proved effective, just as he said it would. The moans subsided, the jerking and writhing stopped and like every other child when it is relieved of pain it fell into a deep, easy sleep. The doctor (he had earned the right to be called a doctor) now turned his attention fully to the mother. He took her pulse and checked her carefully, looking intently into her eyes. The look made her body shudder and her heart shrink because the gaze was so familiar and yet it was the cold look of a stranger. Finally, satisfied that he had seen all he needed to see he mixed another drink.

"I don't know anything about any mythical drink that produces forgetfulness, like Lethe or Nepenthe," he said, "but I have learned many new secrets in the wilderness and this is one of them. An Indian taught me about it in return for some things I taught him that are as old as Paracelsus. Drink it! It may be less soothing than a sinless conscience. That I cannot give you; but it will calm your nerves." He gave her the cup and Hester took it with a slow, earnest look into his face; not exactly a look of fear, but full of doubt and questioning as to what he meant to do. And she stole a look at her sleeping baby.

"I have thought of death," she said, "have wished for it—would even have prayed for it if I had thought that a person like me was fit to pray for anything. Yet, if there's death in this cup I beg you to tell me now before I drink it, because, believe me, that's what I'll do." She raised the cup to her lips.

"Drink it then," he said, as cold and flat as ever. "Do you know me so little, Hester Prynne? Have you ever known my purposes to be that shallow? Even if I wanted to avenge myself on you, do you think I'd kill you? No, I would keep you alive. I'd give you all the medicines that would keep you from harm so that you would continue to live to feel the blazing and burning shame that's marked out on your breast." As he spoke he touched the scarlet letter with his long finger.

Hester felt as if his finger had been red-hot and she reacted to it and he took full notice of it. "Live then," he said with a smile, "and carry your doom around with you before the eyes of men and women. Carry it around before the eyes of him you called husband and in the eyes of that child there. So drink it and you will live."

She argued no more and immediately drained the cup. He motioned her to sit on the bed beside the sleeping child while he brought the only chair in the room near to her and sat in it. She couldn't keep from trembling. He had done all that basic decency or professional principle required of him and now she was sure that he was getting ready to speak to her as the man she had deeply and irreparably injured. But she was wrong.

"Hester," he said, "I don't ask why or how you have fallen into this pit, or how you climbed up on that pedestal of infamy I found you on. The reason's not hard to find. It was my stupidity and your weakness. I'm a man of thought, the bookworm of great libraries, a man already in decay, having given my best years to feed the hungry dream of knowledge—what did I have in common with youth and beauty like yours? I was born misshapen; how could I delude myself with the idea that intellect would make up for physical deformity in a young girl's dreams? Men call me wise. If the wise ever helped themselves I would have foreseen all this. I should have known that when I came out of that vast and dismal forest and back into this settlement of Christian men that the very first object I would see would be you, Hester Prynne, standing up there, shamed before the people. No, long before that, from the moment when we came down the old church steps together as a married pair I should have foreseen this letter blazing at the end of our path." Depressed as she was Hester couldn't endure this last quiet stab..

37

"You know," she said, "you know that I was honest with you. I didn't love you and I didn't pretend to love you."

"True," he said, "it was my stupidity! I've admitted that. But up to that time in my life I'd lived my life in vain. The world had been so cheerless! My heart was a place big enough for many guests but it was lonely and chilly. There was no cozy household fire in it and I longed to have one going there. It didn't seem like a wild dream—even though I was old and gloomy and misshapen—it didn't seem like a wild dream that the simple bliss that the whole of humanity is allowed to share in might still be mine. So I drew you into my heart, Hester, into its innermost chamber and tried to warm you by the warmth that your presence brought to me."

"I have greatly wronged you," murmured Hester.

"We have wronged each other," he responded. "Mine was the first wrong, when I seduced your youth into a false and unnatural relationship with my decay. So, because my years of learning have not been completely useless I'm not looking for vengeance, I'm plotting no evil against you."

"Between you and me," he continued, "the scale hangs fairly balanced. But, Hester," and here his voice took on a terrible intensity, "the man lives that has wronged us both! Who is he?"

"Don't ask me!" Hester Prynne replied, looking him straight in the eye, "You'll never know!"

"Never? Did you say Never?" he leaned back in the chair as he answered with the sinister smile of an intelligent man that was sure of himself. "Never know him! Hmmm, believe me, Hester, there are very few things—in the visible world or, within reason, in the invisible world of thought—that remain hidden from the man that devotes himself to uncover."

"You may hide your secret from the prying crowd, you may conceal it from the ministers and magistrates, as you did today when they tried to wrench the name out of you and give yourself a partner on that pedestal, but I'm not like them! I come to the investigation with senses they don't have."

He leaned forward again and with quiet and awful fervor he said, "I will hunt this man as I have hunted truth in books, as I have searched for gold in alchemy. There's a mutual interest and feeling that will make me sense his presence. I'll see him tremble. I'll feel myself shudder, suddenly and unexpectedly when he's near. Sooner or later he will be mine."

The eyes of the wrinkled old scholar burned so intensely on her that Hester put her hands over her heart, dreading that even as he spoke he might be able to read the secret hidden there.

"You will not tell me his name?" he hissed, "None the less, he is mine. He has no infamous letter sewn into his garment as you do, but I will see it on his heart. But don't be afraid for him! Don't think that I will lay a finger on him and interfere with Heaven's work of punishment or that I will betray him into the grip of the legal system—that would be loss to me! And don't imagine that I will get someone else to kill him or that I will do anything to undermine his fame if he is a person of great reputation. Let him live! Let him hide himself in outward honor if he chooses to. Just the same, he will be mine!"

Hester, both bewildered and horrified, "You act as though you were merciful but your words make it clear as crystal that your deeds are acts of cruelty and terror."

He ignored the remark and said, "One thing I want to lay on you—you who were my wife—you have kept the identity of your lover secret. Keep my identity secret also. Nobody in this country knows me. Don't you breathe as much as a word to any living soul that I was ever your husband."

"I will live here. If I were to go and live anywhere else in this land I would be a wanderer and isolated from human interests but here I find a woman, a man and a child with whom I have the closest bonds, ligaments that tie us together. It doesn't matter if it is love or hate or right or wrong that binds us, we are drawn together. You and yours, Hester Prynne, belong to me. My home is where you are and where he is. But see to it that you don't reveal my identity!"

"Why do you want it this way?" she wanted to know. Afraid to enter the agreement though she didn't really know why. "Why not make it public and cast me off immediately?"

He said, "It might be because I will avoid the dishonor that would cling to me, the husband of a faithless wife. It might be for many reasons. Never mind why, it's my purpose to live and die unknown. So let the world think that your husband is already dead and that he will never be heard of again. Don't ever show that you recognize me, not by word or sign or glance! Above all, don't ever breathe a word about me to the man you keep secret. If you fail me in this— beware! His fame, his position and his life will be in my hands. Beware!"

Hester said, "I will keep your secret as I have this kept this one."

"Swear it!" he hissed. And she took the oath.

"And now Mistress Prynne," said old Roger Chillingworth, as he would be known from that time forward, "I leave you alone, alone with your infant and the scarlet letter. Tell me, Hester? Does your sentence demand that you wear the scarlet letter in your sleep? Are you not afraid of nightmares and hideous dreams?"

"Why are you smiling at me this way?" she asked, deeply troubled by the look in his eyes. "Are you the Evil Spirit that haunts the forest around us? Have you enticed me into an oath that will ruin my soul?"

He answered, with another smile, "Not your soul. No, not yours."

5

Hester at her Needle

Hester Prynne's term of confinement was now at an end. Her prison-door was thrown open, and out she came into the sunshine. She felt sick and morbid at heart and thought the sun shone on everyone without exception for no other purpose than to reveal the scarlet letter on her breast. Her first steps of freedom that took her away from the prison door might even have been more torturous than in the public procession and spectacle I described earlier. But she had strength of character and out of it rose the emotional and mental power to battle against such a highly charged situation and turn it into a kind of lurid triumph. She had had to call on all the vital reserves of inner strength to get through it.

Besides, though the effort on that single occasion demanded more emotional strength from her than she would have used up in many quiet years, it was a single event that she would never have to face again. Then there was this, on that occasion the very law that condemned her had held her up on its strong arm through the terrible ordeal, protecting her against an unbridled public and spelling out the limit of punishment. It was a sort of giant with stern features, you see, and while it had the power to humiliate her it also had the power to support her. But that was then, now that she was free and walked away from the prison door unsupported by the law, the daily grind had begun and she was on her own. She must carry on living each day by the ordinary resources of her nature or sink beneath the weight. She could no longer borrow from the future to help her through the present grief as a prisoner can look forward to a day when the punishment ends. But in Hester's case the future held no promise of relief.

Tomorrow would bring its own trial and so would the next day and the next: each with its own trial and yet the very same burden that was now so unutterably grievous to bear. She'd toil on toward the far-off future with a burden she would never be able to fling down, and it would grow heavier because the coming days and years would pile up their misery on the enormous heap of shame. During all that time she would no longer be a person but a general symbol for the preacher and moralist to point at to illustrate and embody their images of woman's frailty and sinful passion. In this way the young and pure would be taught to look at her as the figure and the body, the reality of sin, with the scarlet letter flaming out its message. They'd be taught to look at her—at her, the child of honorable parents—at her, the mother of a baby that would later be a woman—at her, who had once been innocent. And over her grave, the infamy that she must carry there would be her only monument.

She wasn't required by law to stay within the limits of the Puritan colony, a region remote and obscure. She was free to go anywhere she wanted. Home perhaps to where she was born or to some European city where she could begin a new life with her past safely hidden away. She might have gone into the forest and lived among those that did not live by the law that condemned her, but she chose to remain. That seems an incredible decision for the woman to make, that she should still call this place her home, since here it was inevitable that she would remain a monument to shame. Had she moved elsewhere this wouldn't have been the case.

But for so many people there's a fatality, a feeling so irresistible and unavoidable that it has the force of doom. It almost invariably compels human beings to linger around and haunt, like a ghost, the spot where some great and marked event has given the color to their life; and the darker the tinge that saddens it the more irresistible it seems to be. Her sin and her dishonor were the roots she had struck into the soil. To every other pilgrim and wanderer this forestland might have seemed unfriendly but not to Hester Prynne. With her sin, her life seemed to have begun here rather than in another place and long ago. Wild and dreary or not, it was her home. All other places on earth were foreign to her in comparison to this one. Even that village of rural England where she had been happy as a child and pure as a girl now seemed to be her mother's home—it was foreign to her; home was where she now lived. The chain that bound her here was of iron links and though they galled her inmost soul they were unbreakable.

But there was more than that! Although she hid the secret even from herself, and grew pale whenever it struggled out of her heart, like a serpent from its hole—there was something else that kept her in that area. Here lived and here walked the feet of one she considered herself joined to in a union that was unrecognized on earth. While it was not recognized on earth because it was not a marriage union, it was the kind of union that would bring them together before the bar of final judgment. And, in a sense, that bar would be the altar at which they would "marry" and be joined in endless retribution. She was riddled with guilt and expecting nothing but eternal punishment but at least she and her lover would be together forever. Over and over again, the tempter of souls had thrust this idea into Hester's thoughts and laughed as he watched her. With passionate and desperate joy she seized the thought and then agonized to get it out of her mind.

She barely looked the idea in the face before hurrying to shut it up in its dungeon.

What she compelled herself to believe—what, finally, she concluded was her motive for continuing to be a resident of New England—was half a truth and half a self-delusion. Here, she said to herself, had been the scene of her guilt and here should be the scene of her earthly punishment. In this way perhaps the torture of her daily shame would at length purge her soul, and work out another purity in the place of the one she had lost: a purity more saintly because it would be the result of this living martyrdom. That's why she didn't leave.

On the outskirts of the town, within the verge of the peninsula but well away from any other house, there was a small thatched cottage. An earlier settler had built it and then abandoned it because the soil around it was too sterile for cultivation. It was somewhat isolated because that was the habit of immigrants— they built their houses well away from others because they wanted to avoid much social activity. It stood on the shore looking across a basin of the sea at the forest-covered hills, towards the west. A clump of scrubby trees that were peculiar to the peninsula didn't so much hide the cottage from view, they seemed to suggest that here this object would like to remain—or should remain—out of sight. In this lonely little house, with such slender means as she possessed and by the license of the magistrates who still kept an inquisitor's eyes on her, Hester established herself with her infant child. The spot immediately came to have a sinister and mysterious reputation and air. Children, too young to understand why this woman should be shut away from human fellowship and warmth would creep near enough to watch her working her needle at the cottage-window. Or they'd watch her standing in the doorway, working in her little garden or coming along the pathway that led to the town, and having noted the infamous scarlet letter they'd scamper off with a strange contagious fear.

Hester's situation was truly lonely and without a friend on earth who dared to show himself but she was never in danger of being utterly destitute. She had a gift with a needle that got her enough work to provide food for her and the baby even in a land where there's wasn't a great demand for needle-work. She bore on her breast, in the curiously embroidered letter, a specimen of her

47

delicate and imaginative skill. The dames of a court would have been very pleased to get her to do work for them because she could add splendor and ingenuity to their fabrics of silk and gold. It's true that in the darker simplicity of the Puritan way of dressing not many would call for the finer products of her handiwork but times were changing and changing tastes were gaining influence even over our stern ancestors.

Of course, as a matter of policy, public ceremonies were marked by stately and well-conducted ceremonies. Ordinations or the installation of magistrates so gave importance and majesty to the forms in which a new government paraded before the people. These occasions required a sober but yet a studied magnificence and Hester was more than able to create it. Deep ruffs, painfully wrought bands, and gorgeously embroidered gloves—these were all necessary to the men of high office. Such things were allowed also to individuals if they were dignified by rank or wealth; though there were laws related to luxurious dressing that the common people kept to. In the steady stream of funerals there was a frequent and characteristic demand for the kind of work that Hester Prynne could produce. It didn't matter if it was for the clothing of the dead or for the bereaved so that they could express their sorrow in various ways in ebony cloth or snowy linen, Hester was more than capable. Baby-linen also generated jobs and income for her, because babies then as now wore royal robes.

By degrees, but more quickly than you might have been expected, her handiwork became what would now be termed the fashion. It isn't clear why the people came to her. Perhaps it was out of commiseration for a woman of so miserable a destiny. Or it may have been from the morbid curiosity that gives a fictitious value even to common or worthless things. As the pen that was once owned by a murderer or a chair that a witch once sat in had a special appeal.

Vain people might have chosen to "mortify" themselves at public ceremonies of pomp and state by wearing something made by her sinful hands. Others might have been drawn to her because she had become what they had tried and failed to become—"famous". But it might have been that Hester really did supply a need and fill a gap that would otherwise have remained vacant. This much is certain: she had as many hours employment with her needle as she was prepared to undertake and when she did take on a job she did it wonderfully.

Her needle-work was seen on the ruff of the Governor; military men wore it on their scarves, and the minister on his band; it decked the baby's little cap and when the dead were buried in their coffins her work was buried to mildew and molder away along with them. But there is not a record of a single case where her skill was called on to embroider the white veil that was to cover the pure blushes of a bride. The exception indicated the ever-relentless vigor with which society frowned on her particular sin.

Hester had no real interest in getting anything beyond the very basic needs; the plainest and most ascetic things were enough for her and a simple abundance for her child. Her own dress was of the coarsest materials and the dullest color; it had only one ornament— the scarlet letter. The child's clothing, on the other hand, was extravagant ingenuity that actually matched and underlined the wild exuberance that developed early in the little girl. But it had a deeper meaning that I will speak later. Except for that expenditure and their basic needs Hester gave to charity and to wretches less miserable then herself any other income. What she got in return from many of them was insult. Much of the time that she could easily have spent making the finer things she spent in making coarse garments for the poor. The driving force behind all this was penance and though she obviously enjoyed the work she wouldn't permit herself to approve of the pleasure. She had a sensuous nature and took pleasure in the lush and the lovely and it showed in her work—her passionate needlework was her only outlet.

To Hester Prynne it must have been a way of expressing and therefore soothing the passion of her life but like all other joys she rejected it as sin. I am afraid that this morbid troubling of the conscience with a matter of no consequence implied no genuine and steadfast penitence, but something doubtful, something that might be deeply wrong within.

Because she found no joy in anything and because of her morbid conscience Hester Prynne came to have a part to perform in her world. With her natural energy, character and rare gifts society could not entirely cast her off though it had set its awful mark on her. There was nothing in all her dealings with society that made her feel as if she belonged to it. By every gesture, every word and even by their silence, every person she met implied or expressed that she was banished. She was as much alone as if she inhabited another planet or that she had no way of communicating with the inhabitants of this world. She was a ghost that revisits the familiar fireside but can't make itself seen or felt; a ghost that can't smile along with the household joy or mourn with the family sorrow. She was a ghost that, even if it should succeed in showing its sympathy, would only terrorize those who see it and drive them off.

She expressed no interest in moral matters for how could such a sinner claim to be interested in moral issues? She had to pretend such things didn't matter to her even while she was deeply concerned with them. The only way she functioned in the hearts of those around her was to generate their fears and bitterest scorn. It wasn't an age of delicacy! She understood her place very well and was in no danger of forgetting it but they often reminded her of it—a mirror shoved in front of her face, new anguish generated by the rudest touch on the tenderest spot. I mentioned already that even the poor she went looking for, to do them good, even they often despised the hand that stretched out to support them. It was no different with the dames of elevated rank whose houses she entered when they employed her. They never forgot to distil drops of bitterness into her heart, sometimes through that witchcraft of quiet malice by which people can concoct a subtle poison from ordinary trifles. Sometimes the insults were subtle, like a needle painfully, slyly and expertly inserted and at other times the vile expressions on her defenseless head were a rough blow on an ulcerated wound. What a wondrous use of power this is to mercilessly beat those that can't hit back. And how ingenious we are when we need to come up with good reasons to do such things. But Hester had schooled herself long and well and she never responded to these attacks except by a flush of crimson that spread from her cheek to her breast. She was patient—a martyr, in fact, but not so much a martyr that she chose to pray for the forgiveness of

51

her enemies in case instead of a blessing her pain led her to curse them instead.

Continually, and in a thousand different ways she felt the throbs of anguish brought on by the undying and ever-active sentence of the Puritan tribunal.

Clergymen paused in the streets to address words of exhortation that brought a grinning and frowning crowd around the poor sinful woman. If she entered a church, hoping to share the Sabbath smile of the Universal Father she found herself the text of the sermon. She grew to dread children for they had absorbed from their parents a vague idea of something horrible in this dreary woman that glided silently through the town with never any companion but a child. They would allow her to pass and then they'd pursue her at a distance with shrill cries, using a word that had no distinct meaning for them but was even more terrible to her precisely because it came from lips that babbled it without understanding.

Here was irrational contempt! And when even little children tormented her it seemed to her that her shame was known everywhere by everyone and by everything. All nature knew of it. It could have caused her no deeper pain if the leaves of the trees had whispered the dark story among themselves, if the summer breeze murmured about it or if the wintry blast had shrieked it aloud! She felt a peculiar torture in the gaze of a new eye—now someone else knew. When strangers looked curiously at the scarlet letter and none ever failed to do so— they branded it afresh in Hester's soul so that, often, she could scarcely keep herself from covering the symbol with her hand (but she never did). But then, again, the eye of someone who knew the story well had its own anguish to inflict.

When she might have expected that familiarity would lead to a milder reaction the continued icy cold stares told her she was still repulsive and the pain of it was barely tolerable. In short, from first to last, Hester Prynne knew that a human eye was always on the scarlet letter so the spot never grew callous; on the contrary, it seemed to grow more sensitive with daily torture.

But sometimes, once in many days or maybe in many months, she felt an eye—a human eye—on the shame-filled brand that seemed to give a momentary relief, as if half of her agony were shared. The next instant, back it all rushed again, with an even deeper throb of pain because in that moment by feeling relief she felt she had sinned again. She had no right to ease or understanding or pity.

To look for these or to approve them when they came on rare occasions lessened her guilt, you see, it made her sin not so sinful and that was more unbearable than the pain.

Her imagination was somewhat affected, but if she had been of a softer moral and intellectual fiber she would have been affected even more by the strange and solitary anguish of her life. Alone in the little world with which she was outwardly connected it seemed to Hester now and then that the scarlet letter had gifted her with a new sense. Even if it was only in her imagination it was still too powerful to resist. Imagination or not it's what she felt. She shuddered to believe, yet couldn't help believing, that it gave her knowledge of the hidden sin in other hearts because she was feeling what they were feeling. She was terror-stricken by the revelations that were made in this way. What were they? Were they the insidious whispers of a bad angel, anxious to persuade the struggling woman, still only half his victim, that the outward appearance of purity was nothing but a lie? Should she welcome cynicism and give it a home in her heart? Should she make less of her own sin because everyone else was sinning in the same way? Could it be that if the truth about everyone were to be revealed that a scarlet letter would blaze forth on many a bosom besides Hester Prynne's? Must she receive that inner foreboding—so obscure, yet so distinct—as truth? In all her miserable experience, there was nothing else so awful and so loathsome as this sense. It perplexed, as well as shocked her when she had such an experience. Sometimes the letter on her breast would give a sympathetic throb as she passed, with eyes down, near a venerable minister or magistrate, the model of piety and justice. "Some evil thing is near?" Hester would say to herself and lifting her reluctant eyes there would be no one there but this earthly saint! She would often feel she had a sister in sin nearby and then meet the holy frown of some matron, who according to what everyone said, had kept cold snow in her heart all through her life. That frozen snow in the matron's bosom and the burning shame on Hester Prynne's—what had the two in common? Or, the tingling vibration would warn her, "Look Hester, here is someone just like you. She'd make a suitable companion for you!" And looking up she would catch a young maiden glancing at the scarlet letter, but shyly and slyly. Then she'd quickly turn away with a faint crimson in her cheeks as if her purity had been stained a bit by that momentary glance. Such loss of faith is always one of the saddest results of sin for with it comes the great temptation to see the whole world as polluted.

Whatever else she thought this much is true Hester Prynne—the victim of her own moral weakness and man's hard law— believed that no one in the world was guilty as she was guilty or sinful as she was sinful.

The crude in those dreary old times were always attaching a grotesque horror to what seized their imaginations and they had a story about the scarlet letter which we might easily work up into a terrific legend. They vowed that the symbol was not mere scarlet cloth, tinged in an earthly dye-pot but was red-hot with infernal fire and that it could be seen glowing whenever Hester Prynne walked abroad in the nighttime. I'm compelled to say that it seared Hester's bosom so deeply that perhaps there was more truth in the rumor than our modern incredulity may be inclined to admit.

6

Pearl

Up until now we've hardly spoken of the infant, that little creature whose innocent life that had by some immutable decree of Providence sprung up as a lovely and immortal flower out of the rank luxuriance of a guilty passion. Hester watched the child's astonishing growth in beauty and intelligence with astonishment of her own. Her Pearl—that's what Hester had called her; not because it described her appearance, which had nothing of the calm, white, unimpassioned luster that that would suggest. She named the infant "Pearl," because she was of great price—purchased with all she had—her mother's only treasure! It's strange isn't it, that Man had marked this woman's sin by a scarlet letter that had such disastrous power while Providence, as a direct consequence of the sin that man punishes, had given her a lovely child and placed her on that same dishonored bosom to shape her for eternal life. Yet these thoughts filled Hester Prynne less with hope than fearful expectation. She knew her deed had been evil so she couldn't believe that its result would be good. Day after day she looked fearfully into the child's expanding nature, always dreading that she might see in her some dark and wild peculiarity that would echo and highlight the sin that led to her birth—would she do what her mother did? Certainly there was no physical defect. Looking at its perfect shape and poise the infant might have been born in the Garden of Eden. The little girl had an inborn grace and manual skill that doesn't always accompany faultless beauty.

Her mother, with a morbid purpose, bought the finest materials that could be got and allowed her rich imagination its full play and dressed the child in splendor when they were in the public eye. But while it's true that she looked magnificent when dressed like that, it wasn't the clothes that made her. The gorgeous dresses might have outshone the loveliness of some others that wore them but not Pearl, this was a very beautiful child. And even if she was in a dull gown, torn and soiled she looked just as radiant. She was flushed with the mystery and glory of infinite variety; in this one child there were many children, all the way from the wild-flower prettiness of a peasant-baby to the small-scale pomp of an infant princess. Central to the child's make up and permeating it all there was a passion, a certain depth of color that she never lost; take that away and Pearl would no longer have been Pearl! Her outer nature expressed the complexities of her inner life. She was deep as well as varied but—unless Hester's fears deceived her—the child lacked something of critical importance. She didn't take into account the world she was born into. She could not be made submissive or agreeable to rules. Her life began in a defiance of law and rules and the result was a puzzle whose pieces though beautiful and brilliant were all put together in disorder. Perhaps there was a peculiar order but if so, it was one that was hidden under the mass of unbridled variations. Hester's wild guesses could only account for the child's baffling character by recalling what she had been and felt during that passionate and chaotic experience when Pearl was getting her soul from the spiritual world and her bodily frame from two that were very much of the earth. And then the mother's high-strung state during the troubled days that followed transmitted to the unborn infant the lines within which its moral and emotional life would run.

And however white and clear the elements in her were originally, they had taken the deep stains of crimson and gold, the fiery luster, the black shadow and the dazzling light of the new elements that were now Pearl. Above all, the warfare of Hester's spirit during that time was perpetuated in Pearl. She could recognize her wild, desperate, defiant mood, the flightiness of her temper and even some of the very cloud-shapes of gloom and despondency that had brooded in her heart. As a young child's disposition they could be held in check and balanced out to some degree but later in life they could result in storm and whirlwind.

The discipline of the family in those days was of a far more rigid kind than now. The frown, the harsh rebuke, the frequent use of the stick or rod, ordered on the grounds of Scriptural authority, were used not merely to punish actual offenses but as a wholesome regimen for the growth and promotion of all childish virtues. Hester Prynne, the loving mother of this one child, ran little risk of being unduly severe but she knew her own errors and misfortunes so she sought early to impose a tender but strict control over this child committed to her charge. But the task was beyond her skill. After testing both smiles and frowns and proving that neither approach possessed any measurable influence, she stood aside and allowed the child to be swayed by her own impulses. Physical compulsion or restraint worked of course—while it lasted. As to any other kind of discipline, whether addressed to her mind or heart, it all depended on Pearl's mood at the time, so it might or might not make any difference. Her mother came to know a certain peculiar look on Pearl's face, even in early infancy, that warned her when it was pointless to insist, persuade or plead.

Intelligent or not sometimes the look was malicious but usually it was a wild flow of spirits. There were times when Hester wondered if Pearl was a human child. She seemed more like a fragile elf with a mocking smile. A look appeared in her wild, bright, deeply black eyes and clothed her with a strange unearthliness. Was she a vapor, hovering in the air that could vanish at any moment or a glimmering light that comes out of nowhere and then is gone? Too superstitious, when she saw that look Hester would rush to the child, press her close and kiss her earnestly. It wasn't overflowing love, it was to assure herself that Pearl was flesh and blood and not something else. And the way the child laughed—it was merry and musical but there was something else to it. Something the mother couldn't pinpoint.

Heart-smitten at this bewildering and baffling spell that so often came between her and this treasure that she had bought at so great a price Hester sometimes burst into sobbing. There was no way to know how her tears might affect the child. Sometimes she would frown, clench her fist and harden her features into a stern and unsympathetic look of discontent and often she would laugh again, and louder than before, like a thing incapable of feeling or understanding human sorrow. She was much too old to be so young. Or—but this more rarely happened—sometimes she would be convulsed with grief and sob out her love for her mother in broken words and seemed intent on proving that she had a heart by showing it was breaking. But that tenderness that was like a gust of wind and passed as suddenly as it came so it gave no comfort to the mother. Brooding over all these matters, she felt like someone who had brought up a spirit in a seance but, because she didn't perform the ritual just right, she had failed to gain control of this new and unpredictable presence. The only real peace she got was when the child lay in restful sleep. Then she was sure of her and tasted hours of quiet, sad, delicious happiness; until—perhaps with that perverse expression beginning to show from beneath her opening lids—Pearl awoke! It was remarkable how quickly the child arrived at an age when she was capable of social intercourse and outgrew her mother's ever-ready smile and nonsense-words! Once that had happened Hester would have been thrilled if she could have heard the child's talking and laughing with other children but this would never be. Pearl was born to live cut off from a child's world. An imp of evil, the sign and product of sin and she had no right among christened infants. The instinct with which the child grasped her loneliness and came to terms with the destiny that had drawn an unbreakable circle round about her came to her early.

She fully sensed where she stood with other children. Never since her release from prison had Hester met the public without her. In all her walks about the town, Pearl was with her. First as the babe in arms and afterwards as the little girl, the small companion of her mother; holding a forefinger with her whole grasp and tripping along at the rate of three or four steps to one of Hester's. She saw the children of the settlement on the grassy margin of the street, or at the doors of their houses, showing themselves in as grim a manner as their puritanical shaping would permit! There they were, maybe playing at going to church or at scourging Quakers or taking scalps in a sham fight with the Indians or scaring one another with shows of pretended witchcraft. Pearl saw, watched intently but never tried to make a friend. She wouldn't answer if someone spoke to her.

Sometimes the children would gather round her and Pearl would grow positively terrible in her puny wrath, snatching up stones to fling at them, with shrill, incoherent yelling that made her mother tremble because they had so much the sound of a witch's curses in some unknown language.

The little Puritans, being part of the most intolerant brood that ever lived, had got a vague idea of something uncanny and unearthly in both the mother and child. They scorned them in their hearts and gouged them with their words. Pearl felt all this and gave it back with the bitterest hatred that a child can drag up.

These outbreaks of fierce temper were valuable and even comforted the mother because she could at least make sense of them. They were earnest and honest moods instead of the fitful caprice in the child's behavior that so often grieved and confused her. Still, it appalled her to see again a shadowy reflection of the evil that had existed in herself. All this enmity and passion Pearl had inherited by inalienable right out of Hester's heart. Mother and daughter stood together in the same circle of seclusion from human society and Hester reminded herself daily that her sin had robbed Pearl of all social fellowship.

At home, within and around her mother's cottage Pearl didn't want a wide circle of acquaintances. She communicated life to a thousand objects the way a torch starts a fire whenever it touches things. The unlikeliest materials—a stick, a bunch of rags, a flower—these were the puppets of Pearl's witchcraft, and while they still looked the same she made them serve a place in whatever drama she had in her mind. A multitude of imaginary people, old and young, could speak through that one baby-voice of hers. She turned the aged black and solemn pinetrees and their melancholy groans in the wind into Puritan elders and the ugliest weeds of the garden were their children. These she crushed or unmercifully uprooted. Her attention span was short; one moment she would dart up and dance or lie as if asleep but with mind whirling. She was always in a state of extraordinary activity—soon sinking down, as if exhausted by so rapid and feverish a tide of life—and then following that by other explosions of a similar wild energy. It was a phantasmagoric play of the Northern Lights. All this imagining was no different than what we see in other children of growing and bright minds except that Pearl was more dependent on her visionary creations because she lacked friends. What was strange here was that Pearl disliked all her creations.

She never created a friend, as in the ancient myth she sowed nothing but dragon's teeth from which sprang a harvest of armed enemies, against whom she rushed to battle. It was inexpressibly sad; what depth of sorrow must a mother have felt in her heart when she saw in one so young this constant awareness that the world was hostile? Especially when the mother held herself responsible for it all. And how sad to see how the child disciplined her energies to engage in a war that would inevitably come.

Often Hester Prynne would look at Pearl and dropping her work on her knees she would cry out with an agony she couldn't suppress and somewhere between speech and a groan she would pray. "O Father in Heaven—if you are still my Father—what is this being that I have brought into the world?" And Pearl, either overhearing or aware in some more subtle way of her anguish, would turn her vivid and beautiful little face on her mother, smile with gremlin-like intelligence and resume her play.

There is one more thing about this child and her behavior that requires mention. Babies normally first notice their mother's smile and respond to it with something of a smile of their own, or at least, something that is thought to be a smile (the kind of thing fond parents argue about, was it or was it not a responsive smile?). But that's not the first thing Pearl seemed to notice. It was the scarlet letter on Hester's bosom! One day as her mother leaned over the cradle the infant's eyes had been riveted by the sight of the glimmering gold embroidery around the letter. And putting up her little hand she grasped at it, smiling; not a look that might have been a smile, but with a definite gleam that gave her face the look of a much older child. Hester gasped for breath and grabbed at the fatal token, instinctively, trying to tear it away. The pain inflicted by the knowing touch of the baby's hand was excruciating. And there it was again; as if her mother's agony-filled gesture were meant only to entertain her, the baby girl looked into her eyes and smiled. From that defining moment, except when the child was asleep, Hester never felt a moment's peace or a moment when she could calmly enjoy her. Sometimes weeks would pass by before Pearl would eye the scarlet letter; but then, out of the blue, it would come again, like the stroke of sudden death, and always with that ghastly smile and odd expression of the eyes.

Once when she was looking into her child's eyes, as mothers are fond of doing, trying to see herself in them, that eerie and elfish look came into the child's eyes. Suddenly, because women in solitude and with troubled hearts are harassed with delusions that come from who knows where, Hester thought she saw a face looking back at her in the small black mirror that was Pearl's eye. It wasn't her own miniature portrait but another face. It was a fiend's face, full of smiling malice. But it bore all the features of a familiar face, one that she had come to know full well, though it had seldom smiled and never shown malice.

Had an evil spirit possessed the child and had just then peeped out in mockery? Many a time afterwards that same delusion tortured Hester though never so vividly as then.

In the afternoon of a certain summer's day when Pearl had grown big enough to run about, she amused herself with gathering handfuls of wild flowers, and flinging them, one by one, at her mother's bosom. She would dance like a dervish whenever she hit the scarlet target. Hester's first impulse had been to cover her breast with her clasped hands but she resisted. Whether from pride or resignation or a feeling that her repentance would best be worked out by this unutterable pain, she sat erect, pale as death, looking sadly into her wild eyes. The barrage of flowers kept coming, almost invariably hitting the mark, and covering the mother's breast with hurts that nothing in this world could soothe and if there was some cure in another world Hester didn't know how to find it. At last, when all her ammunition was done the child stood still and gazed at her mother with that laughing image of a fiend peeping out from the fathomless abyss of her black eyes. Or so it seemed to the mother.

"Child, what are you?" cried the mother.

"Oh, I am your little Pearl!" answered the child. But while she said it, Pearl laughed, and began to dance up and down with the capricious and wild gestures of an imp whose next bizarre act might be to fly up the chimney.

"Are you really my child?" asked Hester. At that moment she asked the question in earnest because Pearl's behavior was so perceptive and so in touch with her social standing that it appeared she knew everything. Hester half believed that she knew the whole story and at any moment might pour it out.

"Yes; I am little Pearl!" repeated the child, continuing her antics.

"You are not my child! You are no Pearl of mine!" probingly and only half playfully. "Tell me, then, what you are, and who sent you here?"

"Tell me, mother!" said the child, seriously, coming up to Hester, and pressing herself close to her knees. "You tell me!"

"Your Heavenly Father sent you!" answered Hester Prynne.

But she said it with a hesitation that didn't escape the girl. Whether she was moved only by her usual strangeness or because an evil spirit prompted her, she put up her small forefinger and touched the scarlet letter.

"He did not send me!" she said with determination. "I have no Heavenly Father!"

"Hush, Pearl, hush! You mustn't talk that way!" the mother answered, suppressing a groan. "He sent us all into the world. He sent even me, your mother so I know he sent you! Or, if not, you strange and elfish child, tell me where did you come from?"

"Tell me! Tell me!" repeated Pearl, no longer seriously, but laughing and capering about the floor. "It's you that must tell me!" But Hester could not resolve the query and continued to torment herself in a dismal labyrinth of doubt. She remembered—between a smile and a shudder— the talk of the neighboring townspeople who had tried in vain to identify the child's father. They had noted some of her odd ways and had started the rumor that Pearl was a demon's child. Stories from ancient times told of demons that had been seen on earth and that by using a sinful woman they produced a child to promote some foul and wicked purpose. Luther, according to the scandal of his monkish enemies, was a brat of that hellish breed and Pearl wasn't the only child the New England Puritans claimed had a demonic father.

7

The Governor's Hall

Hester Prynne went one day to the mansion of Governor Bellingham, with a pair of gloves that she had fringed and embroidered the way he had ordered. He was to wear them on some great occasion of state, because despite the fact that a popular election had lowered him a step or two from the highest rank he still held an honorable and influential place among the colonial magistracy.

But Hester had a far more important reason to want an interview with so powerful a person in the affairs of the settlement. Certainly she wasn't there simply to deliver a pair of embroidered gloves. She'd heard that some of the leading and more rigid religious citizens were purposing to deprive her of her child! Taking the view that Pearl was of demonic origin these good people not unreasonably argued that it was their Christian duty, in the interest of the mother's soul to remove such a stumbling-block from her path. If the child, on the other hand, were really capable of moral and religious growth and possessed the elements of ultimate salvation, then it was important to transfer her to wiser and better guardians than Hester Prynne. Bellingham was one of the ring-leaders that promoted the action. At this late date it might seem both strange and a bit ludicrous that an affair of this kind that could have been dealt with by some select men of the town should have been a question of public policy and one on which statesmen of eminence took sides. But in that age of pure simplicity, matters of even lesser public interest and of far less intrinsic importance than the welfare of Hester and her child were often part of the deliberations of legislators and acts of state. It was only a little while before the time of our story that a dispute about the ownership of a pig not only caused a fierce and bitter contest in the legislative body of the colony but also resulted in an important modification of the framework of the legislature itself.

She was worried, but Hester Prynne set out from her cottage because she was so conscious of her being in the right that being a solitary woman against the public didn't seem to her to be an unequal match. Pearl went with her of course. She could run easily by her mother's side and since she was constantly in motion from morn till sunset she could easily have made a much longer journey than one to the Governor's house. But being spoiled and self-willed and not because she needed it she demanded that she be carried; no sooner was she picked up than she demanded to be let down again.

She was dressed in a crimson velvet tunic of a peculiar cut, embroidered in fantasies and flourishes of gold thread. It was so well adapted to the girl's complexion and beauty that it made her the very brightest little jet of flame that ever danced on the earth.

But what was most remarkable about the child's clothes, in fact, of the child's whole appearance, was that it irresistibly and inevitably reminded those that saw her of the token that Hester Prynne also wore. The child was the scarlet letter in another form: the scarlet letter endowed with life! The mother herself—as if the red shame were so deeply scorched into her brain that all her thoughts were shaped by it—had lavished many hours of morbid ingenuity to make Pearl look as vibrant and alive as the badge of her shame. To her it made some kind of sense because Pearl was the one as well as the other, the one she loved and the fruit of her sin.

When the two of them came to the outskirts of the town the Puritan children took note and stopped their play—or what passed for play with those sober children.

"Look, there's that woman and her scarlet letter along with her! Come on..." and the mud started to fly.

But this wasn't a child that could be intimidated. She glared at them and then rushed—they scattered to the four winds. She was an infant pestilence—the scarlet fever, or some soon-to-graduate angel of judgment—whose mission was to punish the sins of the rising generation. She screamed and shouted as she ran to them and they ran from her. It wasn't just her temper that drove them off—she had the advantage of a satanic reputation.

71

Governor Bellingham's house was a large wooden structure, the old-fashioned kind that's still seen occasionally in the streets of our older towns. Now it was moss-covered, crumbling to decay and inside it was melancholy at heart from missing the joyful events that once took place in the now empty rooms. But on the other hand there was the cheerfulness that streams from a house into which death has never entered. It really did have a very cheery look about it. The walls that weren't moss covered were spread with a kind of stucco in which fragments of broken glass were mixed so that, when the sunshine glanced off the front of the building it glittered and sparkled as if someone had flung handfuls of diamonds against it. It was bright enough to have been Aladdin's cave rather than the mansion of a grave old Puritan ruler. And it was decorated with strange cabalistic figures and diagrams, drawn in the stucco when it was newly laid on and they were suitable to the quaint taste of the age. Pearl, looking at the bright wonder of the place began to caper and dance and insisted that the whole breadth of sunshine should be stripped off its front and given to her to play with.

"No, child," said her mother; "Gather your own sunshine. I have none to give you!" They approached the arched door that was flanked on each side by a narrow tower both of which had lattice-windows with wooden shutters. Lifting the iron hammer door-knocker Hester Prynne signaled that she'd arrived and the knock was answered by one of the Governor's bond servants—a recently arrived and free-born Englishman, but now a seven years slave. During that term he was to be the property of his master and as much a commodity of bargain and sale as an ox or a joint-stool. He wore the usual regalia of serving-men at that period; a custom brought over from the old hereditary halls of England.

"Is the worshipful Governor Bellingham in?" Inquired Hester.

"He is indeed," the bondservant said, staring with wide-open eyes at his first sight of a scarlet letter.

"Yes, his honorable worship is in. But he has a godly minister or two and a doctor with him. You may not see him now." "Nevertheless, I will enter," the woman answered and the bondservant offered no opposition, judging that she was a great lady in the land from the authoritative way she carried herself and the glittering symbol on her dress.

So the mother and child were admitted into the hall of entrance.

Bellingham had modeled his new house after the houses of the wealthy and aristocratic in his native land. There was a wide and reasonably lofty hall, extending through the whole depth of the house connecting more or less directly, with all the other apartments. The windows that formed a small recess on either side of the portal lighted one end of this spacious room. At the other end, though partly muffled by a curtain, it was more powerfully lit up by one of those bay hall windows, which we read about in old books, and which was provided with a deep and cushioned seat and literature for guests wishing to browse. The furniture of the hall was Elizabethan in style and consisted of some ponderous chairs with elaborately carved backs of wreaths of oak flowers, and there was a table in the same taste. Heirlooms, no doubt, brought over from the Governor's family home. On the table—indicating that old English hospitality had not been left behind—stood a large pewter tankard and if they'd looked in Hester or Pearl would have seen the frothy remains of a recent draught of ale.

On the wall hung a row of portraits; the forefathers of the Bellingham line; some wearing armor and others with stately ruffs and robes of peace. They all were characterized by the sternness and severity that old portraits invariably showed, glaring with harsh and intolerant criticism at the pursuits and enjoyments of living men.

A modern suit of armor hung on the paneled oak wall among all the ancient and forbidding pictures. A skilled craftsman in London made it especially for Governor Bellingham in the same year he came over to New England. There was a steel head-piece, a cuirass, a gorget and greaves, a pair of gauntlets and a sword hanging underneath. It was all (especially the helmet and breastplate) so highly burnished that it glowed with white radiance under the light and scattered it, dazzling all over the floor. This shining armor was not for mere show; Bellingham had worn it on many a solemn gathering and, more to the point, at the head of a regiment in the Pequot War. For though he had trained as a lawyer and was accustomed to speak of Bacon, Coke, Noye and Finch as his professional associates, the emergencies and necessities of this new country had transformed Governor Bellingham into a soldier as well as a statesman and ruler.

Pearl was as taken with the gleaming armor as she had been with the glittering frontispiece of the house and spent some time looking into the polished mirror of the breastplate.

"Mother," she shouted, "I see you here. Look! Look!" To humor the child she looked and saw that owing to the peculiar effect of this convex mirror that the scarlet lettering now looked huge; making it by far the most prominent feature of her appearance. The truth is, she seemed to be absolutely hidden behind it. The girl pointed upwards also, at a similar picture in the headpiece, smiling at her mother with that almost malicious look on her child's face. That grinning look was reflected in the mirror also and it so deeply affected Hester that she felt that it couldn't be her own child that looked up at it but some spiteful imp that molded itself into Pearl's shape.

"Come along, Pearl," she said, pulling her away, "let's look in the garden and see what flowers are there. There might be even more beautiful ones than we find in the woods." The girl ran to the bow window at the further end of the hall, and looked the length of the garden walk that was carpeted with closely cut grass and bordered with some rude and immature attempt at shrubbery. But it seems the owner had already given up as a hopeless job any attempt to raise an English garden in the hard soil of New England. Cabbages grew in plain sight. There was a pumpkin-vine, rooted at some distance that had run across the intervening space and deposited one of its gigantic products directly beneath the hall window. It was as if it were telling the Governor that this great lump of vegetable gold was as rich an ornament as New England earth would offer him. There were a few rose-bushes and a number of apple-trees (probably the descendants of those planted by the Reverend Mr. Blackstone, the first settler of the peninsula; that half mythological person who rides through our early records seated on the back of a bull).

As soon as Pearl spotted the rose bushes she began to whimper for one and her mother couldn't make her stop.

"Hush, child—hush!" her mother hissed at her. "Please stop crying! I hear voices in the garden. The Governor's coming and gentlemen along with him." Coming down the garden path she saw a number of people approaching the house. In utter scorn of her mother's attempt to quiet her, Pearl gave a bad-tempered scream and then became silent. The silence was no attempt to please; it was just that she had caught sight of the visitors coming along the garden path so now there was something new to focus her attention and curiosity.

8

The Elf-Child and the Minister

Governor Bellingham, in a loose gown and easy cap—the kind that elderly gentlemen used to love to wear around the house—was taking his visitors around his estate. The big ringed and elaborate ruff, beneath his gray beard, in the antiquated fashion of King James's reign, made his head look like John the Baptist's on a plate.

His appearance was rigid and severe, almost "frost-bitten," due to late age and severe religion but his way and his religion didn't seem to match up with all the worldly and pleasure-bringing things he surrounded himself with. Still, it's a complete misunderstanding of our great forefathers to think they made it a matter of conscience to avoid pleasant things, luxuries even, if they were within their grasp. It's true they spoke about human existence as hardly anything but trial and warfare but not everyone thought that way though many of them were willing to sacrifice possessions and life if duty called for it. The venerable pastor John Wilson whose beard, white as a snowdrift, could easily be seen behind Governor Bellingham never taught this stern ascetic creed. Nurtured at the rich bosom of the English Church the old clergyman had a long established and legitimate taste for all good and comfortable things. And however stern he seemed in the pulpit or in his public reproof of transgressions like that of Hester Prynne's, his genial benevolence in private life had won him warmer affection than any of his professional colleagues.

Behind the Governor and Mr. Wilson came two other guests. One was the Reverend Arthur Dimmesdale, whom I mentioned earlier as having taken a brief and reluctant part in the scene of Hester Prynne's disgrace and close beside him was old Roger Chillingworth.

You will remember that he was a person of great skill in medicine and had come to this town from the forests two or three years earlier. It was public knowledge that this learned man was the physician as well as friend of the young minister whose health had recently deteriorated as a result of too much self-sacrifice connected with the labors and duties of his pastoral position.

The Governor, in advance of his visitors, climbed a few steps and throwing open the leaves of the great hall window found himself almost falling over little Pearl. The shadow of the curtain fell on Hester Prynne and partially concealed her.

"What have we here?" said Governor Bellingham, looking with surprise at the little scarlet figure in front of him. "I confess I've never seen the like of it since my days in old King James's time when I thought it was marvelous to be allowed into the court wearing a mask.

"There used to be a swarm of these small apparitions in holiday time and we called them children of the Lord of Misrule. But how did such a guest get into my hall?"

"Aye, indeed!" cried good old Mr. Wilson. "What little bird of scarlet plumage may this be? I think I have seen figures like this reflected on the floor when the sun has been shining through a richly painted window. Tell me, young one, who you are and how come your mother dressed you in this strange way? Are you a Christian child—huh? Do you know your catechism? Or are you one of those naughty elves or fairies that we thought we had left behind us in merry old England with other Papish relics?"

"I am mother's child," answered the scarlet vision, "and my name is Pearl!"

"Pearl?—Ruby, perhaps—or Coral!—or Red Rose, at the very least, judging from the color of you!" responded the old minister, stretching out to pat her cheek. But she would have none of it.

"But where is this mother of yours? Ah! I see," he added, because it had just dawned on him and turning to Governor Bellingham he whispered, "This is the very child of whom we spoke together, and that's the unhappy woman, Hester Prynne, her mother!"

"You don't say?" cried the Governor.

"No, we might have thought that such a child's mother would be a gaudy prostitute like the Whore of Babylon! Still, the timing is good, and we will look into this matter here and now." Governor

Bellingham stepped through the window into the hall, followed by his three guests.

"Hester Prynne," he said, fixing his naturally stern gaze on her, "there has been much discussion about you lately. One point in particular we have discussed at great length and very seriously. We have been debating whether those of us of authority and influence are doing well by our consciences when we trust an immortal soul, such as there is in that child there, to the guidance of someone who has stumbled and fallen in the pitfalls of this world. So, speak up, you are the child's own mother! Do you not think it would be better if she were taken out of your charge, dressed soberly, disciplined strictly and instructed in the truths of heaven and earth? What can you do for the child in these matters?"

"I can teach my little child what I have learned from this!" answered Hester Prynne, laying her finger on the red token.

"Woman, it is your badge of shame!" replied the stern magistrate.

"It is precisely because of the stain that that letter bears witness to that we would transfer the child to other hands."

"Nevertheless," said the mother, calmly, though growing paler, "this badge has taught me—it daily teaches me—it is teaching me at this moment—lessons by which my child may be the wiser and better even if they can bring no profit to myself."

"We will judge carefully," said Bellingham, "and reflect well on what we are about to do. Good Master Wilson, please, if you would, examine this Pearl—since that is her name—and see if she has had such Christian nurture as we would expect in a child of her age."

The old minister seated himself in an armchair and made an effort to draw Pearl between his knees but the child wasn't accustomed to being touched by anyone but her mother. She ran out through the open window and stood on the upper step, looking like a wild tropical bird of rich plumage, ready to fly away. Mr. Wilson was clearly startled by this response because he was a grandfatherly sort of person and usually a great favorite with children. But he attempted to proceed with the examination.

"Pearl," he said, with great solemnity, "you must take heed to instruction so that in due time, you may wear in your heart the pearl of great price. Can you tell me, my child, who made you?" Now Pearl knew well enough who made her. Her mother began to teach her things about earthly fathers shortly after she had told her about her Heavenly Father. In any case, Pearl had ten thousand questions and like every curious child she had asked questions on that subject. And Pearl on anyone's estimate was no ordinary child; that was clear. She had come so far in her three years that she could have borne a fair examination in the New England Primer or the first column of the Westminster Catechisms though she had never even glimpsed either of those celebrated works. But there's a perversity that appears in all children to some degree and Pearl had ten times her share. Now, at the worst possible moment, it took thorough possession of her. She closed her lips or deliberately talked nonsense. She was rude and difficult and several times refused to answer the question at all. Then putting her finger in her mouth, the child finally announced that she had not been made at all but had been plucked by her mother off the bush of wild roses that grew by the prison-door.

This precocious child had probably created the fantasy on the spur of the moment and got the suggestion from the Governor's red roses that stood near by, just outside of the window. And, there was of course, her recollection of the prison rose bush, which they had passed in coming here.

Old Roger Chillingworth, with a smile on his face, whispered something in the young clergyman's ear. Hester Prynne looked at him and even then, with her fate hanging in the balance, she was startled to see the change that had come over his features. How much uglier they now were and his dark complexion seemed to have grown gloomier and his figure more misshapen—since the days when she first knew him. She met his eyes for an instant but immediately had to give all her attention to the scene in front of her.

"This is awful!" cried the Governor, recovering slowly from the astonishment that Pearl's response had thrown him into. "Here is a child three years old and she cannot tell who made her! Without question, she is equally in the dark as to her soul and its present depravity and future destiny! Gentlemen, I don't think we need inquire any further." Hester caught hold of Pearl and drew her forcibly into her arms, confronting the old Puritan magistrate with almost a fierce expression.

Alone in the world, cast off by it and with this sole treasure to keep her heart alive, she felt that she possessed indisputable rights against the world and she was ready to defend them to the death.

"God gave me the child!" she shouted. "He gave her in the place of all else that you had taken from me. She is my happiness—and she is my torture none the less! Pearl keeps me here in life! Pearl punishes me, too! Do you not see she *is* the scarlet letter, but she's capable of being loved. And because both those things are true she has all the more power to punish me for my sin because the very sight of her reminds me daily of my sin! As long as I love her I cannot be without her and as long as I have her I have the living reminder of what I have done. But I lover her and you will not take her from me! I will die first!" "My poor woman," said the not unkind old minister, "the child shall be well cared for—far better than thou can do for it." "God gave her into my keeping!" repeated Hester Prynne, raising her voice almost to a shriek. "I will not give her up!" And then by a sudden impulse, she turned to the young clergyman, Mr. Dimmesdale, though she seemed hardly to have known he was there for she never even glanced at him. "You speak for me!" she cried into his face. You were my pastor and had charge of my soul, and you know me better than these men can. I will not lose the child! Speak for me! You know—for you have sympathies that these men lack— you know what is in my heart, and what a mother's rights are, and how much the stronger they are when that mother has no one but her child and the scarlet letter! Look to it!" And with a desperate and very deliberate, almost a hiss she said, "I... will... not... lose... the... child! Look you to it!"

At this wild and strange appeal, which indicated that Hester Prynne's situation had provoked her to near madness, the young minister at once came forward, pale, and holding his hand over his heart, as was his custom whenever his peculiarly nervous temperament was thrown into agitation. He looked now more careworn and emaciated than he had appeared at the scene of Hester's public shaming; and whether it was his failing health or whatever the cause might be, his large dark eyes had a world of pain in their troubled and melancholy depths.

"There is truth in what she says," began the minister, with a voice sweet, tremulous, but powerful, so that the hall re-echoed and the hollow armor rang with it—"truth in what Hester says, and in the feeling which inspires her! God gave her the child, and gave her, too, an instinctive knowledge of the child's nature and requirements—both are obviously so peculiar. That means the mother is better suited to care for her than anyone else would be. And, of course, there is this, is there not a quality of awful sacredness in the relation between this mother and this child?"

"Ay—and how is that, good Master Dimmesdale?" interrupted the Governor. "Make that plain, if you please!"

"It must be so," resumed the minister. "For, if we deny it, do we not imply that the Heavenly Father, the creator of all flesh, has made no distinction between unhallowed lust and holy love and in doing that, wouldn't it mean he has made light of sin? This child of its father's guilt and its mother's shame has come from the hand of God to work in many ways on this woman, who pleads so earnestly and with such bitterness of spirit the right to keep her. God meant the child as a blessing—for the only blessing in her life! And no doubt, as the mother herself has told us, it was for retribution also, a torture to be felt at many an unexpected moment; a pang, a sting, an ever recurring agony in the middle of a troubled joy! Has she not expressed this thought in the way she dresses the poor child, so forcibly reminding us of that red symbol which sears her heart?"

"You put that very well," Mr. Wilson said. "I confess that I had thought the woman had no better intention than to make a freak and an offense out of her child!"

"Oh, not so!—not so!" continued Mr. Dimmesdale. "Believe me, she recognizes the solemn miracle that God has worked in the life of that child. And may she feel, too—what I think is the very truth—that this gift was meant, above everything else, to keep the mother's soul alive, and to preserve her from blacker depths of sin into which Satan might otherwise have plunged her! So I think it's good for this poor, sinful woman that she have an immortal child, a being capable of eternal joy or sorrow, given into her care. She is to train her to righteousness and this will ceaselessly remind the mother of her fall and at the same time teach her, as if it were by the Creator's sacred pledge, that if she brings the child to heaven the child also will bring its parents there! In that regard the sinful mother is in a more fortunate position than the sinful father is. For Hester Prynne's sake, then, and no less for the poor child's sake, let us leave them as Providence has seen fit to place them!"

"You speak, my friend, with a strange earnestness," said old Roger Chillingworth, smiling at him.

"And there is great weight in what my young brother has spoken," added the Rev. Mr. Wilson.

"What do you think, worshipful Master Bellingham? Has he not pleaded well for the poor woman?"

"Indeed he has," answered the magistrate; "and he has brought out such good arguments that we will leave the matter as it now stands. Providing, you understand that there will be no further scandal in the woman. Just the same, we need to see to it that the child is appropriately examined in the catechism at stated times. This should be done by you Mr. Wilson or by Master Dimmesdale. And in addition, at the proper time, the tithing-men, in good standing in the church must see to it that she goes both to school and to church meetings."

The young minister, when he had finished speaking had withdrawn a few steps from the group, and stood with his face partially concealed in the heavy folds of the window-curtain. His shadow on the floor was trembling with the depth of feeling in his appeal. Pearl, wild and flighty up to now, stole softly towards him and taking his hand in both her own laid her cheek against it. It was such a tender caress and done without pretense or attempt to impress—as if there was no one there to impress—that her mother who was looking on asked herself, "Is that my Pearl?" She knew of course that there was love in the child's heart, though it mostly revealed itself in a spirited passion. Not twice in her lifetime had she seen it softened by such gentleness as now. The minister looked around and seeing her, laid his hand on the child, hesitated only a moment and then gently kissed her head. There are not many things a minister seeks that are sweeter than the gentle and high regard of women. But among those things is the innocent child's instinctive pleasure in his presence, because it seems to imply that there is something in him that is truly worthy to be loved.

But Pearl's unusual mood lasted only for a moment before she laughed and went capering down the hall so airily that old Mr. Wilson wondered if even her tiptoes touched the floor.

"The little baggage has witchcraft in her, I think," he said to Mr. Dimmesdale. "She doesn't need an old woman's broomstick to fly!"

"A strange child!" remarked old Roger Chillingworth. "It's easy to see the mother's part in her. Would it be beyond a philosopher's research, do you think, gentlemen, to analyze that child's nature and from it make a mold that would give us a shrewd guess at the father?"

"No, it would be sinful, in such a situation to follow the clue of profane philosophy," said Mr. Wilson. "Better to fast and pray about it; and it might be better still to leave the mystery as we find it unless Providence for its own reasons chooses to reveal it. That leaves it open for every good Christian man to have the privilege to show a father's kindness towards the poor, deserted little thing."

The whole affair being so satisfactorily concluded, the relieved Hester Prynne and her daughter left the house. Some people say that as they went down the steps the lattice of a chamber-window was thrown open and out of the shadows and into the sunny day Mistress Hibbins, Governor Bellingham's bitter-tempered sister, thrust her ugly face. This is the woman that only a few years later was executed for being a witch.

"Hist, hist!" she called, her head jutting out like some evil gargoyle seemed to cast a shadow over the cheerful exterior of that part of the house. "Will you go with us to-night? There will be a merry company in the forest and I just about promised the Dark One that the beautiful Hester Prynne would be part of the group."

"Make my excuse to him if you like!" Hester called back, with a triumphant smile. "I'm staying at home and keeping a close watch over my little Pearl. If they had taken her from me, I would willingly have gone with you into the forest and signed my name in the Dark One's book too. Yes, and I would have done it with my own blood!"

"We shall have you there before long!" said the witch-lady, with a disappointed frown as she disappeared behind the window again.

But here—if we take this exchange between Mistress Hibbins and Hester Prynne to be authentic—was already an illustration of the young minister's argument against tearing the fallen mother from the child that came from her sinful weakness. Even at this early stage the child saved her mother from Satan's snare.

9

The Leech

The reader will remember that under the name of Roger Chillingworth another name was hidden; a name he would never use again. I told you that in the crowd that witnessed Hester Prynne's shameful exposure there was an elderly man, travel-worn and just emerging from the wilderness. He saw the woman in whom he had hoped to find the warmth and cheerfulness of home publicly paraded as a model sinner. Her status as a wife was trodden into the ground and her infamous reputation was on every mouth in the marketplace.

If the news ever reached her family or her close friends they would feel the weight of the guilt and the shame, and the more intimate and sacred the relationship was the greater the contagion of her dishonor would be. All that being so, why would this individual come forward to vindicate his claim to an inheritance like that? He was not going to be made a fool of and he certainly wasn't going to stand beside her on her pedestal of shame. The only one that knew him was Hester Prynne and you'll remember how he intimidated her into an oath of silence. He withdrew his name from the roll of mankind and vanished out of life as completely as if he lay at the bottom of the ocean; which is where rumor had long ago said he was. Having closed one door he now opened another. The door led into the dark and he willingly, even eagerly, chose it. There might not have been guilt involved in opening that door but there was certainly darkness, and there was enough force and drive in that dark choice to engage his full strength and mind. He had a sinister agenda.

To gain what he was going after he took up residence in the Puritan town as Roger Chillingworth, with no other introduction than his learning and intelligence; and he possessed more than a common measure of those. His studies earlier in life meant that he was thoroughly and widely acquainted with the medical science of the day. So he presented himself as a physician, and as such he was cordially received because skilful men of the medical and surgical profession were rare people in the colony. It's true, or so it appeared, that men that worked in these areas were seldom moved by the religious zeal that brought other emigrants across the Atlantic; and it's possible that their researches into the human frame killed their interest in other subjects. When physical causes were discovered for phenomena that once were explained by spirit causation then perhaps it isn't surprising that medical men began to assume that all was to be explained that way. It could be that they became so engrossed in the mechanical wonders of the human body that they lost all interest in any supposed realm, concluding that the totality of life was mechanical. In any case, the health of the good town of Boston needed a skilled doctor. Until Chillingworth's arrival the town's health lay under the protection of an aged deacon and a chemist, whose piety and godly behavior were the only strong testimonials in his favor because he had no diploma. There was a resident "surgeon," but he was the local barber who occasionally tried his hand at the noble and exalted art of operating on bodies instead of hairs. Every medical remedy the pair had was concocted and compounded with a seriousness that suggested they were handling the Elixir of Life and they put into all of them a multitude of far-fetched and variously originating ingredients. To such a professional body Roger Chillingworth was a brilliant acquisition and he soon showed that he was familiar with the ponderous and imposing machinery of antique medicines. While he had been captive to the Indians he had added a great deal to his stock of knowledge about the properties and power of native herbs and roots. And he openly insisted with his patients that as far as he was concerned these simple medicines, Nature's gift to the untutored savage, were as good as the European Pharmacopoeia that so many learned doctors had spent centuries to build up.

In the outward forms of a religious life this learned stranger was exemplary and soon after his arrival he had judiciously chosen for his spiritual guide the Reverend Dimmesdale. The young divine whose scholarly renown still lived on in Oxford was considered by his more fervent admirers as little less than a heavenly ordained apostle.

Everyone knew that if he lived long enough he was destined to do great deeds for the now feeble New England Church just as the early Fathers had achieved much for the Christian faith in its infancy. But, sad to tell, it was about this time that the health of Mr. Dimmesdale had clearly begun to fail. Those who knew him best insisted that he worked much too hard and long. His deep devotion to study and his conscientious fulfillment of his pastoral duties were the reason for the paleness on the young minister's cheek. But more than all else, his failing health resulted from the fasts and vigils he constantly engaged in. He practiced these to keep his heart closely in tune with God and to keep his human limitations from obscuring his vision of that Lord; but it was clear that he was injuring himself as the saintly Francis of Assisi had done. There were those who insisted that if Mr. Dimmesdale was really going to die it was because the world wasn't a worthy enough place for him to live in any longer. But, of course, with his characteristic humility he fervently claimed that if Providence should see fit to remove him it would be because of his own unworthiness to perform its humblest mission here on earth. Debate may have raged as to why he was declining but there could be no question of the fact of it. His form grew gaunt and wasted and his voice, though still rich and sweet, had a certain melancholy prophecy of decay in it. On any slight alarm or moment of distress he had got into the habit of putting his hand over his heart. He would flush at first and then go pale—he was obviously in great pain.

This was the young clergyman's condition and it would have come as no surprise to the townspeople if the young man's dawning light went out entirely despite the fact that he was a young man. It was at that point that Roger Chillingworth arrived in the town.

If he had dropped down out of the sky or simply risen up out of the earth his coming would have been no more of an enigma because no one had the faintest notion where he came from. This gave his arrival something of a mysterious nature and it wasn't far from there—at least in the minds of some and by numerous colorful retellings—for his entry to become embellished with the miraculous. He was now known to be a man of skill; people noticed that he gathered herbs and the blossoms of wild flowers and dug up roots and plucked off twigs from the forest like someone acquainted with virtues that were hidden from ordinary mortals. He was heard to speak of Sir Kenelm Digby and other famous men whose scientific attainments were thought to be almost supernatural. And when he talked about them he spoke of them as having been his correspondents and associates. Why, since he was so esteemed and established in the learned world had he come to this place? It was obvious that he belonged to the great cities and established universities, what was his business in the wilderness? A rumor gained ground in answer to this question and however absurd it might sound some very sensible people believed it.

Heaven had wrought an absolute miracle by transporting an eminent Doctor of Medicine from a German university bodily through the air and set him down at the door of Mr. Dimmesdale's study! Individuals of wiser faith who knew that Heaven promotes its purposes without aiming at the stage-effect called miraculous intervention, were still quite prepared to see a providential hand in Roger Chillingworth's perfectly timed arrival.

This idea was given firmer support when people noticed the strong interest that the physician always showed in the young clergyman. He attached himself to him as a parishioner and sought to win friendship and confidence from this naturally private and reserved young man.

He expressed great alarm at his pastor's state of health but was anxious to attempt the cure. He even thought if it were undertaken without delay that he might be able to turn things around for the young minister. Of course, being the brilliant man he was and having arrived in the nick of time, he had the full and unceasing support of the elders, the deacons, the motherly dames and the young and fair maidens of Mr. Dimmesdale's flock. Mr. Dimmesdale, however, gently repelled their entreaties.

"I need no medicine," he insisted.

But how could the young minister say so, when, with every successive Sabbath, his cheek was paler and thinner and his voice more tremulous than before? How could he say so when it had now become a constant habit, rather than a casual gesture, to press his hand over his heart? Was he weary of his labors? Did he wish to die? These questions were solemnly put to him by the elder ministers of Boston and the deacons of his church, who, to use their own phrase, "dealt with him," on the sin of rejecting the aid which Providence so manifestly held out. He listened in silence and finally and reluctantly promised to confer with the doctor.

When he finally spoke to Chillingworth it was reluctantly. He said, "If it were God's will I would be well content if my labors and my sorrows and my sins and my pains should shortly end with me. I would be well satisfied if what is earthly of them was buried in my grave and the spiritual go with me to my eternal state rather than have you expend your time and energy and skill on my behalf."

"Ah," replied Roger Chillingworth, with that quietness that was characteristic of him, "this is the way that a young clergyman is apt to speak. Youthful men, not having taken a deep root, give up their hold on life so easily! And saintly men, who walk with God on earth, would like to be away, to walk with him on the golden pavements of the New Jerusalem."

"No," rejoined the young minister, putting his hand to his heart, with a flush of pain flitting over his brow, "if I were worthy to walk there I could be better content to toil here."

"Good men are always too hard on themselves," said the physician.

That is how the mysterious Roger Chillingworth became the medical adviser of the Reverend Mr. Dimmesdale. But he was interested in more than the disease for he was the kind that looked into the heart and mind of the patient so the two men, so different in age, came gradually to spend a lot of time together. For the sake of the minister's health, and to allow the doctor to gather plants with healing balm in them, they took long walks on the seashore or in the forest. And they often visited in one another's house. The young minister was fascinated with the man of science because of the depth of his intellect and the wide range and freedom of ideas that he would never have found among the members of his own profession.

You must understand that Mr. Dimmesdale was a true priest, a true man of faith. His reverence was well developed and the structure of his mind drove itself powerfully along the track of a definite creed that deepened as time passed. No one anywhere would have called him a man of liberal views. He was so constructed that it would always be essential to his peace to feel the pressure of a faith about him, supporting him even while it confined him within its iron framework—he was a conservative and a traditionalist. All that is true, but he experienced the thrill of pleasure and relief when now and then he had the opportunity to look at the universe through the eyes of an "outsider" rather than those he normally dealt with. It was as if a window were thrown open, allowing fresh air into the stuffy and stifled study where his life was wasting away in the lamp-light and the musty odor that comes from old books. But the air was too fresh and chilly to be breathed with comfort for very long by his orthodox lungs, so both minister and physician drew back within the limits of what their Church defined as orthodox.

In this way Roger Chillingworth got to scrutinize his patient carefully. He saw him both in his ordinary life, keeping to an accustomed path in the range of thoughts familiar to him, but he also saw how he reacted when he was thrown into ethical and moral situations that might call something new to the surface of his character. He held it to be a basic medical truth that the diseases of the physical frame are affected by the peculiarities of that heart and mind. In Arthur Dimmesdale, thought and imagination were so active and sensitivity was so intense that the bodily infirmity would probably have its basis there. So Roger Chillingworth—the kind and friendly physician, delved deeper into his patient's heart, going down among his principles, prying into his recollections and probing everything with a cautious touch, like a treasure-seeker in a dark cavern.

Few secrets can escape an investigator, who has opportunity and license to undertake such a quest and has the skill to follow it up. A man burdened with a secret should especially avoid the intimacy of his physician. If the doctor has natural wisdom and shrewdness and a nameless something more, let's call it intuition, he will learn secrets.

Of course it's fundamentally important that the investigator is pleasant and doesn't rub his patient the wrong way. If he has the power—and it must be born with him—to bring his mind into harmony with his patient's mind—that is, to be empathetic— then he can draw the patient into saying more than he knows he is saying. Such a doctor or confidant will know how to use, not only spoken phrases, but also silence, a breath without words, or perhaps an appropriate single word here and there. In the presence of such a counselor the patient will say things he is sure he only thought. And since this is a professional (which is an additional advantage) a moment will come when the sufferer's whole soul will be dissolved and flow out in a dark but transparent stream, bringing all its mysteries into the light of day.

This is inevitable! Roger Chillingworth possessed all or most of the attributes above.

Nevertheless, though intimacy developed between these two cultivated minds so that their exchanges ranged far and wide no secret stole out of the heart of the young minister. They discussed every topic of ethics and religion, of public affairs and private character; they talked much on both sides about matters that seemed personal to themselves and there was still no sign of the secret that the physician was sure was hidden in the man. On top of that, it occurred to Chillingworth that he had never truly learned even the nature of Dimmesdale's bodily disease. That was very strange, for why on earth would you keep from your doctor knowledge of the very thing you wanted him to heal? Things weren't moving fast enough for the doctor but more to the point, he still wasn't able to watch him as closely as he wanted. So at a hint from him the friends of Mr. Dimmesdale worked it out that the two men were lodged in the same house. The idea being, as the skillful man made clear, that he could keep an even closer, tireless and devoted eye on the poor suffering minister. Naturally the townspeople were thrilled when this was worked out; nothing could have been better for him than this. Well, perhaps what some people in authority continued to insist might even be better—the minister might select one of the many blossoming young women that were spiritually attached to him and make her his devoted wife. But this was out of the question because Arthur Dimmesdale rejected all suggestions of that kind as if priestly celibacy were one of his articles of Church discipline. So he was doomed by his own choice to eat his tasteless morsels always at someone else's table and to endure the life-long chill of one who wants no cozy and warm fireside of his own.

In light of all that, this wise, experienced, benevolent old physician, with both his paternal and reverential love for the young pastor was the very man to be constantly within reach of him.

The two friends moved into the house of a pious widow of good social rank, whose house covered pretty nearly the whole site on which the venerable structure of King's Chapel has since been built.

She lovingly assigned to the young man a front apartment with a sunny exposure and heavy window-curtains to create a noontide shadow when he needed it. There were tapestries hung around the walls telling the scriptural story of David and Bathsheba and Nathan the Prophet. The colors were still bright but Bathsheba looked almost as grim as the woe-announcing seer, which hardly seemed to fit in with the biblical narrative of lust, seduction and compliance. In any case, that was where the pale clergyman piled up his library, rich with parchment-bound folios of the Fathers, the lore of Rabbis and monkish erudition. These were the class of writers and works that the Protestant divines vilified and belittled but continued to use and learn from.

On the other side of the house old Roger Chillingworth arranged his study and laboratory. A modern man of science would think it intolerably incomplete but it was provided with a distilling apparatus and the means of compounding drugs and chemicals, which this practiced alchemist easily turned to his purpose. The two learned men settled themselves into these pleasing and spacious surroundings. Each had his own domain but they became comfortable with one another, frequently looking in on the other man's business without becoming pests.

As you would imagine, the best and wisest friends of the Reverend Arthur Dimmesdale's thought that Providence had done all this for the purpose of restoring the young minister to health. After all, that's what they asked for in so many public, family and private prayers. But there was more to be said about all this! Another section of the community had lately begun to take its own view of the relationship between Mr. Dimmesdale and the mysterious old physician. When the rank and file forms its judgment, as it usually does, on the intuitions of its great and warm heart, the conclusions it draws are often so profound and so unerring that you would think it was truth supernaturally revealed. In this case the people couldn't justify their prejudice against Roger Chillingworth by any fact or argument worth taking seriously so the case against him was more of an impression that filled the air.

It's true there was one very old craftsman who had been a citizen of London at the period of Sir Thomas Overbury's murder, some thirty years earlier; he testified that he saw the physician under some other name, one he couldn't remember. He said the doctor was then in company with Dr. Forman, the famous old conjurer, who was implicated in the Overbury affair. And there were two or three individuals who hinted that during his Indian captivity the old man had enlarged his medical attainments by joining in the incantations of the savage priests. Now everyone knew that these priests were powerful enchanters, often performing seemingly miraculous cures by their skill in the black art. A large number—and many of these were persons of such sober sense and practical observation that their opinions would have been valuable in other matters—a large number affirmed that Roger Chillingworth's appearance had undergone a remarkable change since he had come to town. This was especially marked since he had gone to live with Mr. Dimmesdale. At first, his expression had been calm, meditative and scholarly. Now there was something ugly and evil in his face, something they hadn't previously noticed and which grew still more marked each time they saw him. This deepening ugliness with its suggestion of evil was very unsettling.

According to the crude ideas that began to circulate, the fire in his laboratory had been brought from the lower regions and was fed with infernal fuel and that this was having its effect on his features.

To sum up the matter, popular opinion came to be that the Rev. Arthur Dimmesdale, like so many other persons of special sanctity in all ages of Christian history, was haunted either by Satan himself or Satan's emissary in the guise of old Roger Chillingworth. This diabolical agent was given Divine permission for a limited period to burrow into the clergyman's favor and to plot against his soul.

Naturally, no sensible man doubted who would be the victor in the end but that they were sure that that was what was going on. The people looked with unshaken confidence to see the minister come out of the conflict transfigured with the glory that he would unquestionably win.

Just the same, in the meantime it was sad to think of the possible mortal agony through which he must struggle towards his triumph.

And if the gloom and terror in the depth of the poor minister's eyes was anything to judge by, the battle must have been a sore one and the victory anything but certain.

10

The Leech and his Patient

Throughout his life old Roger Chillingworth had been calm in temperament and kindly, and in all his relations with the world he had been a blameless and upright man though he didn't have it in him to be affectionate. He had begun an investigation to discover the identity of his wife's guilty partner and he was certain that he was conducting it with the impartiality of a judge. He was only after the truth, he told himself, and it had nothing to do with the fact that this unknown person had wronged him. The fact that he had been wounded had no effect on his emotions or his capacity to weigh the evidence, he might as well have been working out a problem in geometry instead of fingering and dissecting human passions and weaknesses. That's what he told himself, but even learned men with great intellects can have vested interests and when those are in play even the intellect is undermined. It isn't that vested interests disable a mind so that it can't work out problems in geometry; but they can blind a mathematical genius so that his reasons for doing geometry or mathematics become twisted. As the physician proceeded, a terrible fascination seized and held him in a vice-like grip and a sort of fierce necessity, a mission, almost a destiny settled down on him. The old man remained emotionally calm and ice cold despite the fever that raged in him from the moment he wakened in the morning until he closed his eyes in dreamy sleep; he was never free again until he had done all its bidding. He dug into the poor clergyman's heart, like a miner searching for possible gold or like a robber plundering a grave in search of a treasure that might have been buried with the corpse. If nothing else, the one thing he was certain to find was crumbling human weakness and corruption and if that's what his soul was driven to find, it only proved that death and corruption didn't wait to be buried—it could be an intellectual dead soul walking.

Sometimes a light glimmered out of the doctor's eyes, burning blue and ominous, like the reflection of a furnace, like one of those gleams of ghastly fire that darted from Bunyan's awful doorway in the hillside and flickered on the pilgrim's face. This obsessed miner loved his work and the tunnels he worked in showed signs of promise, however slight, and that encouraged him. He told himself, "This man has inherited a strong animal nature with all his sensitivity and passion. The very qualities that make him appealing make him vulnerable and as pure as they judge him to be and as spiritual as he seems I need to dig a little farther in the direction of this vein!"

His burning eyes now focused nowhere else but on the young minister whose depths of sympathy, gentleness of spirit and anxiety to please made him the one the needy, lonely and burdened would go to. Chillingworth knew well that the very qualities that make a minister appealing are the qualities that place him in great danger and make him dangerous to others.

But for all his digging all he found were things that were rubbish to him. He uncovered noble dreams that were dreamed for struggling humanity, he found a warm love of souls, pure sentiments and genuine piety that was strengthened by study and intellectual honesty. He wanted none of these and tossed aside treasures that thousands in every generation longed to find and make their own; tossed them aside as obstacles and irritants, as things that were blocking his path to the treasure he really sought. He became stone blind to all but what he was determined to find. At times he would turn back discouraged, but not for long, for in a moment of inspiration he would begin his careful and patient picking and digging in another direction. Patience was needed here because he didn't want to expose his purpose, didn't want the walls to collapse in around him because he dug too eagerly or too anxiously. No thief entered a victim's bedroom more carefully than he sought to creep into the depths of Mr. Dimmesdale and no fraud ever worked more shrewdly to rob his wide-eyed victim of the treasure he guarded with unceasing vigilance. But in spite of his carefulness it was no easy task to enter into the room of a person's mind. Now and then his victim heard the floor creak or a garment rustle or caught a fleeting glimpse of the shadow of a presence, uninvited and much too close for comfort. The intuition, or at least the nerves, of the very sensitive are razor edged and it took almost nothing to make Mr. Dimmesdale vaguely aware that something sinister and deadly to his peace had entered. But old Chillingworth was also sensitivity almost to the point of intuitive. So when the minister turned his startled eyes toward him all he saw was the attentive physician, kind, watchful and sympathizing but never intrusive in any ominous sense. He told himself he must have misunderstood the old man—there was noting sinister there.

Dimmesdale's sick and fearful heart tended to be suspicious of the whole of mankind and while this seemed to protect him best it really left him open to greater danger. He began to doubt his own judgement because he had so often made something out of nothing; he had so often thought someone guilty when they were later shown to be innocent. And so, because he knew that his sickness and fears had disabled him and kept him from trusting any man as his friend, he couldn't recognize his enemy when the enemy actually appeared.

Without his fears, and more to the point, without his self-doubts about his capacity to judge truly, he would have seen through to the obsession that was hidden behind Chillingworth's pretense that he had no other interest than to help. When we add to all that Dimmesdale's willingness to see the best in others, it wasn't surprising that he remained intimate with the old man, inviting him into his study or visiting the laboratory to watch how the doctor turned weeds into potent drugs.

One lovely summer day the minister leaned on the sill of the open window that looked towards the graveyard while the old man examined a bundle of unsightly plants. The minister had gotten into the habit that people burdened with guilt often develop, of avoiding eye to eye contact with people. It wasn't so much that he didn't want to see them directly but more that he wanted no one to see him directly; he wanted no one to enter him through his eyes.

"Where," he asked with a sidelong glance at them, "where my kind doctor did you gather those herbs with the dark, flabby leaves?"

"Just out there in the graveyard," said the physician, without looking up from his work. "They're new to me. I found them growing on a grave that had no tombstone; no other memorial of the dead man except these ugly weeds that have decided to speak for him.

Maybe they grew out of his heart and stand for some hideous secret that was buried with him. If so, he would have done better to confess it during his lifetime."

After a long pause and with a far-away tone, "Maybe," said Dimmesdale, still looking out the window, "maybe he earnestly wanted to but couldn't."

"And why might that be?" said Chillingworth still working away. He was careful to keep his tone just right because he didn't want to give the impression that the matter meant much to him. It was little more than friendly intellectual sparring. "What would keep him from it since all the powers of nature call so earnestly for the confession of sin? Look, don't you think that even these black weeds have sprung up out of a buried heart to make known a crime that hasn't been confessed?"

"That, good sir, is a fantasy of yours," replied the minister, giving no sign that he felt the need to beware. "Nothing but divine mercy can lead to the confession of sin! The confession might take many forms—words or emblems or some such thing—but black weeds don't reveal the secrets of a guilty heart. I believe that such hearts are doomed to hold their secrets until that day when all secrets are revealed, unless God's mercy brings them into the light before then.

Nor do I agree with what you seem to imply, that 'Confession makes everything right.' That seems to say that confession itself is retribution. As I read and interpret Holy Scripture that would be a very shallow view of the matter. No, unless I have missed the mark, one day confession will explain things that aren't understood now. Here and now people often are bewildered by what it is that is going on before their eyes. Confession on that day will answer the many questions they had no answers for in life because they didn't know the whole story. Only complete knowledge of men's hearts can bring full understanding to such problems. And in case you think that the hearts that hold the kind of miserable secrets you speak of will be reluctant to confess them in that day—they won't! Let me tell you, they'll do it with unutterable joy."

"Then why not reveal it here?" asked Roger Chillingworth, slyly stealing a glance at the minister. "Why shouldn't the guilty ones take advantage sooner of this unutterable solace?" Again, carefully maintaining the tone of friendly debate.

"They mostly do," said the clergyman, gripping hard at his chest, as if he were enduring a sharp pain that wouldn't be denied. "Many, many a poor soul has spoken to me in confidence, not only on their death-beds but while strong in life and good in reputation. And oh, the relief I have seen in those sinful brothers immediately after they poured out their hearts. It's as though they had been suffocating and are finally able to draw a breath of clean fresh air. And the

108

experience of relief isn't only momentary, it continues in the days that follow. How can it be otherwise? Why should a wretched man—guilty, we'll say, of murder—why should he prefer to keep the dead corpse buried in his own heart rather than fling it out and let the universe take care of it?"

"Yet some men do bury their secrets that way," observed the calm physician.

"It's true, there are such men. It might be that they keep silent because of their temperament—they lack the inner power to speak so they suppress the burning desire to do it. That seems to me to be one of the more obvious reasons for their silence. But there's surely more to it than that. Why can't we suppose that even though they're guilty they still have a zeal for God's glory and man's welfare? And because of that they don't want to expose themselves publicly as vile and filthy. Once they do that they can achieve no good and the evil of the past can't be redeemed by better service. So, unutterably tormented, they go about among their fellow-creatures looking as pure as new fallen snow while their hearts are all speckled and spotted with iniquity they can't rid themselves of."

"These men deceive themselves," said Roger Chillingworth, with a bit more emphasis than usual, and making a slight gesture with his forefinger as if he were instructing a student. "They fear to take up the shame that rightly belongs to them. Their love for man, their zeal for God's service—these holy impulses may or may not coexist in their hearts with the evil inmates they unbarred the doors of their hearts to.

But it's the nature of this hellish breed that they propagate their kind within such men. If they truly seek to glorify God, these men should not lift their unclean hands to heaven! If they would really serve their fellowmen, let them do it by showing that the power and reality of an honest conscience drives them to penitential and humble self-abasement! Would you have me to believe, my wise and pious friend, that a false show can be better—can be more for God's glory or man's welfare than God's own truth? Trust me, such men deceive themselves!"

"It may be so," said the young clergyman, now with a tone of indifference, as if he were waiving a discussion that he considered pointless to pursue. He was good at escaping from any topic that agitated his too sensitive and nervous temperament. "Now, let me ask my well-skilled physician, if he truly thinks that I have been helped by his kind care of this weak frame of mine?"

Before Roger Chillingworth could answer, they heard the clear, wild laughter of a young child's voice from the graveyard. Instinctively looking out of the open window the minister saw Hester Prynne and Pearl passing along the footpath that crossed the enclosure. Pearl looked as beautiful as the day but she was in one of those tedious moods that led her to think of no one's feelings but her own. She was skipping irreverently from one grave to another, until coming to the broad, flat, tombstone of someone highly-regarded—it might even have been Isaac Johnson himself—she began to dance on it. Her mother commanded and pleaded with her to behave with a bit more consideration and in response Pearl gathered the prickly burrs from a tall burdock that grew beside the tomb. Taking a handful of them she arranged them along the lines of the scarlet letter that decorated her mother's dress. There they clung and Hester made no attempt to pull them off.

Chillingworth had approached the window and smiled grimly down.

"There's no law nor reverence for authority, no regard for human ordinances or opinions, right or wrong, mixed up with that child's character," he said, as much to himself as to his companion. "The other day I saw her splash the Governor himself with water at the cattle-trough in Spring Lane. What in heaven's name is she? Is the little scamp altogether evil? Has she affections? Has she any principle that she lives by?"

"None, except the freedom of a broken law," answered Mr. Dimmesdale, in a quiet way, as if he had been discussing the point within himself. "She lives because holy law was defied and broken. Whether she's capable of good I don't know."

The child probably overheard their voices. She looked up to the window with a bright but couldn't-care-less smile that seemed to have too much wisdom in it and then threw one of the prickly burrs at the Reverend Dimmesdale. The nervous clergyman instinctively jumped back. His frightened response drove her into a fit of laughter and hand-clapping ecstasy. Hester Prynne had involuntarily looked up and all these four persons, old and young, regarded one another in silence until the child laughed out loud and shouted,

"Come away, mother! Come away, or that old demon man will catch you! He has already got hold of the minister. Come away, mother or he'll catch you! But he can't catch me!"

So she drew her mother away, skipping, dancing, and frisking madly among the mounds of the dead, like a creature that owed nothing to a bygone and buried generation and that denied she was even kin to the dead. She was new, had been made fresh out of new elements, and insisted on living her own life and being a law to herself. She refused to have her eccentricities seen as crimes.

"There goes a woman," resumed Roger Chillingworth, after a pause, "who, whatever her sins and failures may be, has none of that mystery of hidden sinfulness that you judge is so grievous to be borne. Do you think Hester Prynne is less miserable because she has that scarlet letter on her breast?"

"Yes, I do truly believe it," answered the clergyman. "Nevertheless, I can't answer for her. There was a look of pain in her face that I wish I hadn't seen. But still, I think it must be better for the sufferer to be free to show his pain—as this poor woman Hester is free—than to cover it up in his heart." There was another pause, and the doctor went back to examining and arranging the plants he had gathered.

"You asked me a little while ago," finally breaking the silence, "for my judgment about your health."

"I did," answered the clergyman. "Please speak frankly whether it is life or death."

"Freely then, and plainly," said the physician, still busy with his plants, but keeping a wary eye on Mr. Dimmesdale, "the disorder is a strange one. Not so much in itself nor even as it shows itself outwardly, at least not in so far as I've observed the symptoms. I've been watching you every day now, my friend, for months and I think you are a man sorely ill. It might be that you are not yet too far gone that a competent and conscientious physician might hope to cure you. But I don't know what to say. Your condition is familiar to me and yet I haven't really come to know what exactly is wrong with you."

"You speak in riddles, doctor," the pale minister said, glancing out of the window.

"Then, to speak more plainly," the physician responded, "and I ask you to forgive me if what I'm about to say seems to need forgiveness because it's too plain. Let me ask as your friend and as one that has been made responsible by God for your life and physical well being, have you told me all I need to know about this condition of yours? Are you keeping anything from me?"

"How can you question it?" asked the minister. "Surely it's child's play to call in a doctor and then hide the sore!"

"You're telling me then that I know everything?" said Roger Chillingworth, deliberately, and fixing an eye, bright and intently focused on the minister's face. "So be it! But again! It's often the case that a doctor that is told only the outward and physical evil only knows half the evil that he's called on to cure. A bodily disease may not be the whole story, it might be only a symptom of some ailment in the spiritual part. I'm again asking your pardon if my speech gives even the shadow of offence. You, sir, of all men whom I have known, are more of a single whole and your body is more in tune with the dictates of your spirit than anyone I have ever encountered."

"Then I need to ask no further," said the clergyman, hurriedly rising from his chair. "You don't deal, I take it, in medicine for the soul!"

"So a sickness," continued Roger Chillingworth, going on as if he hadn't been interrupted, but standing up and confronting the emaciated and white-cheeked minister with his own short, gloomy and misshapen figure. "So a sickness, a sore place in your spirit, if

113

we might call it that, is making its presence known in your bodily frame. Would you want me then, as your physician, to heal the bodily evil? How can I do this unless you first lay open to me the wound or trouble in your soul?"

"No, not to you! Not to an earthly physician!" cried Mr. Dimmesdale passionately, and turning his eyes, full and bright and with a kind of fierceness, on old Roger Chillingworth. "Not to you! But, if my trouble is indeed the soul's disease then I commit myself to the one Physician of the soul! If it suits him he can kill or cure me. Let him do with me as in his justice and wisdom, he sees fit. But who are you to meddle in this matter? Who are you that dares thrust himself between the sufferer and his God?" With a frantic gesture he rushed out of the room.

"You handled this situation very well," Roger Chillingworth said to himself, looking after the minister with a grave smile. "Nothing has been lost. We'll be friends again before too long. But did you see how passion takes hold of this man and drives him out of himself so that he is no longer really himself? If he does that in the heat of one passion he is able to do it in another. He has done a wild thing before now in the hot passion of his heart, this pious Master Dimmesdale."

It didn't prove difficult to re-establish the intimacy they had enjoyed up to this point. The young clergyman, after a few hours of calm reflection on his own, was well aware that he had been highly strung and that that had led to his inappropriate outbreak of temper. Nothing the doctor had said gave him grounds for such an inexcusable outburst. The truth is, he was astonished at the violence with which he had pushed the kind old man away when he was simply offering the advice that went with his job; advice that the minister himself had expressly asked for. So, filled with remorse he lost no time in making a full apology and begged his friend to continue the care which, if it hadn't succeeded in restoring him to health, had in all probability prolonged his feeble existence to that hour. Roger Chillingworth immediately assured him that all was well and that he would go on with his medical supervision of the minister. He did his best for him, in all good faith, but he never left the patient's apartment at the close of the professional interview without a mysterious and puzzled smile upon his lips. He kept the smile from Mr. Dimmesdale of course, but it was there as soon as the physician left the room.

"A rare case," he muttered to himself. "I must look deeper into it. There's a strange and profound sympathy between the soul and the body in this man! If for no other reason than the medical perspective I must get to the bottom of it."

Well one day about noon, not long after the outburst, the Reverend Dimmesdale, without intending to, fell into a deep, deep sleep, sitting in his chair and with a large black-letter volume open before him on the table. It must have been one of those sleep-inducing books of great power that writers keep producing because the minister was a person that slept only fitfully and would jump at the slightest sound or stirring in the air. On this occasion he was dead to the world and didn't stir a muscle when Chillingworth walked into the room. The doctor took no special precautions, there was no tiptoeing or any attempt to conceal his presence and still the young man slumbered.

He walked straight over to his patient and pulled his shirt open.

At that moment Mr. Dimmesdale shuddered and slightly stirred but slept on. In a moment or two the physician turned away. But what a wild look of wonder, joy, and sense of triumph was written all over him! What a ghastly rapture he was experiencing. He was transformed! It was too grand to be expressed only by the eye and the face so it came bursting out through his whole ugly body. He couldn't control himself and delirious with his discovery he was a riot of extravagant gestures; arms were thrown toward the ceiling as he stamped his foot on the floor and hopped around in unbridled jubilation! Had a man seen old Roger Chillingworth at that moment of his ecstasy he would have known without asking how Satan behaves himself when a precious human soul is lost to heaven and won into his kingdom.

The only difference between satanic ecstasy and Chillingworth's was the element of wonder that was in the exultation of this twisted little man. He was astonished.

11

The Interior of a Heart

The relationship between the young Dimmesdale and Chillingworh changed from the moment the old man made his discovery. The conversations sounded the same but they were entirely different though the minister wasn't aware of it. The doctor had worked out a plan of action that was nothing like what he had thought it might be before this startling discovery. His still calm, gentle and clinical exterior hid a quiet but seething depth of happy malice. This capacity had always been there in him but it had remained hidden even to himself, until this astonishing situation gave him the perfect opportunity to express it. This should be no surprise to the reader since it is only when we come face to face with unusual circumstances that we respond in unusual ways and discover things about ourselves that we've never known. The dormant capacity for malevolence was now active in this miserable old man who felt more alive than he had in years. He now had a plan to plan and a purpose to purpose that filled him with a new enthusiasm and got him out of bed in the mornings with a renewed vigor and kept him awake longer at night refining and musing over his next moves. He was imagining a perfectly adapted revenge; one filled with artistry, deft touches and delicate maneuvers that would tax his skill as a wise man to the limits and beyond. He would make himself the one trusted friend of the young man, the one to whom he would confide all his fear, his remorse, his agony, his ineffectual repentance and the inward rush of sinful thoughts that he was sure were gone forever! All that guilty sorrow that the minister kept hidden from the world—a world whose great heart would have pitied and forgiven—all that would be revealed to him, the Pitiless One. To him, the Unforgiving One! All that dark treasure of grief and remorse that would be poured out in an effort to pay the awful debt would be given to the one man among all men on earth who would never count the debt of vengeance as fully paid. Of all men Chillingworth would be the one greedy man that would compound the interest on a debt forever owed.

The clergyman's shy and sensitive reserve continued to thwart this scheme but Roger Chillingworth was patient because the situation was so promising and rich in possibilities. How could he not be pleased? It's true he had adjusted his plans but it was only for the better, for hadn't he received something that was no less than a revelation? It didn't matter to him whether it came from heaven or hell because it transformed his plans and made him more than a spectator of the life of a tortured soul—he was a major actor in it now! He was no longer dealing with merely external things such as flesh and bones. Now he was examining the inmost life and soul of a human being and he was uniquely placed to do it. At times he was delirious with the excitement of it all. He was engaged in more than examination—he had control! He could play him as he chose, like some musical instrument—hit that key and see how it sounds, pluck that string and see what happens. Oh, that one doesn't make the right sound? It isn't sharp enough or sufficiently melancholy? Well, then, try that one! Did he want to make him throb with agony? He knew just what to do or say or hint. The victim was forever on the rack and the doctor knew well what wheel to turn or what spring to release to stretch him till he screamed. Was the skilled man in the mood to startle him with sudden fear? Like a magician waving his wand he'd raise up a thousand grisly phantoms in many shapes—death, more shame, deeper shame, all crowding around this high strung young preacher and pointing their accusing fingers at his chest! Could life be better for the old man, misshapen in body and more twisted in mind? He had a living puppet that could actually feel pain and he was an extravagantly gifted puppet-master. And if it should happen that the doctor wakened in the morning feeling out of sorts he could always take it out on the unsuspecting Dimmesdale.

But was it possible that God was using the avenger and his victim for his own purposes, and, maybe even pardoning where he seemed most to punish? The soft-spoken and sweet-tempered doctor cared nothing for such questions—he had been given a revelation and all relations with Dimmesdale were forever changed.

The consummate actor, he played his part so well that the minister, while he always had a sense that all wasn't well could never put his finger on precisely what it was that caused his unease. It's true that there were times when he looked doubtfully and a little fearfully at the deformed figure of the old physician. He even had his moments when he felt hatred and resentment rise up unbidden. The doctor's gestures, his gait, his grizzled beard, his slightest and most harmless acts, the very way he dressed—all these things sometimes made the clergyman irritable and sick. But he wasn't prepared to admit that these feelings went deeper than the surface because he couldn't give a good reason for the distrust and recoil. The man was respectful, he sounded pious and concerned ("Oh, oh, my dear friend, do you feel all right? Here, sit down and rest. Poor thing, you're having a hard time of it"). The right words came from him with the right inflection and he had the look of one that was anxious only to help. How could anything be wrong when everything was so right? Then there was this, of course, Dimmesdale was fully aware that the poison of one festering and ulcerated spot was infecting his entire life and outlook so he kept coming back to that to explain fully his distant but chronic unease. He took himself to task for those times when he was irritated by and not grateful toward Chillingworth and he did his best to root out the nagging distrust. He couldn't manage that completely so to make up for it he pursued the relationship with the old man. In doing this he bound himself even more tightly to his tormentor. The doctor was hurting the minister but, pathetic creature that he was, with every success he grew more ugly and twisted. Poor forlorn creature— exultant but more wretched than his victim.

Yet, while Chillingworth hated the preacher the people saw the minister as a hero. Despite the bodily disease and torment of his troubled soul and despite the success of the schemes of his deadliest enemy, Dimmesdale's popularity as a minister raced skyward. In fact, it was precisely because of all the troubles and their effect on him that his esteem rose beyond belief.

He won it by his sorrows. His intellectual gifts, his virtues, his power of experiencing and communicating emotion were kept in a state of extraordinary activity by the war in his daily life. He had already risen above even his eminent peers and his reputation was still climbing. There scholars better than Mr. Dimmesdale, men more profoundly versed in solid and valuable attainments than their young colleague. There were stronger minds, gifted with a far greater share of granite doctrinal understanding that meant they were of great value to the church—even if they weren't the most friendly men. And there were the truly saintly fathers who spent time in prayer and spiritual disciplines; men whose purity of life and gentle patience showed that they were more at home in that other world than in this one despite the fact that they still were mortals. All they lacked was the gift that came down on the chosen disciples at Pentecost, in tongues of flame. A symbol, it would appear not so much of the power to speak in foreign languages they didn't know but the power to address the whole human brotherhood in the heart's own language. The words these fathers used came down from the rarefied upper heights where no ordinary mortals live; only the holy fathers habitually dwelt there.

Now it was to this class of men that Dimmesdale truly belonged because that was his nature and tendency. He would have lived on the high mountain peaks of faith and sanctity and he would have continued to climb if he had not been thwarted by the burden of crime and anguish he was doomed to reel and stagger under. It kept him down on a level with the lowest; him, the man of rare spiritual giftedness, whose voice the very angels might have listened for and answered! But it was this very burden that gave him such profound sympathy with and so intimate an understanding of the sinful brotherhood of humanity. His beating heart received their pain and sent its own throb of pain through a thousand other hearts, in gushes of sad and persuasive eloquence. Most often persuasive, but sometimes terrible! The people didn't know the power that moved them as it did. They thought the young clergyman a miracle of holiness. They imagined him the mouthpiece of God's messages of wisdom, and rebuke, and love. In their eyes, the very ground he walked on was made holy. The virgin girls of his church grew pale around him, victims of a passion so filled with religious sentiment that they imagined it to be all religion; they brought it openly and without shame in their white bosoms as their most acceptable sacrifice before the altar. The aged members of his flock, seeing Mr. Dimmesdale's frame so feeble, while they were themselves were so rugged even in their old age, were sure that he'd go heavenward before them.

They told their children that their old bones were to be buried close to their young pastor's holy grave. And all this time poor Dimmesdale, when he thought of his grave, questioned whether the grass would ever grow on it because an accursed thing would be buried there! This public veneration tortured him beyond imagining. His adoration of the truth was genuine and when he said everything but true life with God was shadow and emptiness he meant it with all of his heart. So what did that make him if he had no life with God? He longed to speak out from his own pulpit at the full height of his voice, and tell the people what he was.

"Look at me! In these black clothes of the priesthood; I that climb into this sacred pulpit and turn my pale face to heaven; that dares to take on himself to commune on your behalf with the Most High God. Me in whose daily life you think you see the holiness of Enoch, whose footsteps you think leave a gleam along my earthly track that later pilgrims will be guided home to heaven by. Look at me! I who have laid my hand at baptism on your children, who have breathed the parting prayer over your dying friends at the very moment they were passing from this world and could barely hear the Amen. I, your pastor whom you so revere and trust—I am a pollution and a lie! More than once Dimmesdale had gone into the pulpit with a purpose never to come down its steps until he had spoken words like that. More than once he had cleared his throat, drawn in the long, deep and tremulous breath that would come out burdened with the black secret of his soul.

More than once—no, more than a hundred times—he had actually spoken! Spoken! But how had he spoken? He had told his hearers that he was altogether vile! He had told them that he was viler than the vilest, the worst of sinners, an abomination, a thing of unimaginable sin so that the only wonder was that they didn't see his wretched body shriveled up before their eyes by the burning wrath of the Almighty! Could speech be plainer than this? Why didn't the people jump up out of their seats as if they were one person and tear him down out of the pulpit he had defiled? They heard it all and revered him more. They didn't know what lurked in those self-condemning words. "The godly youth!" they said among themselves. "The saint on earth! Alas! If he sees such sinfulness in his own white soul what horrible spectacles must he see when he looks at you or me!"

Subtle but remorseful hypocrite that he was, the minister knew very well how they would view his generalized confession. By making that kind of open confession of sin he sinned another sin and one he admitted to himself with shame; one he couldn't excuse by saying he was deceived. He had spoken the sober truth but had transformed it into a rotten lie! And yet, he loved the truth and loathed the lie, as few men ever did. And that being true, above all other things that he loathed, he loathed his miserable self! His inner agony drove him to practices more in keeping with the old, corrupted faith of Rome than with the better light of the Protestant church in which he had been born and bred. In Mr. Dimmesdale's secret closet, under lock and key, he kept a blood-covered scourge.

Many times this Protestant and Puritan divine had laid it on his own shoulders, laughing bitterly at himself while he did it, and striking himself so much the more pitilessly because of that bitter laugh. It was his custom, too, as it has been that of many other pious Puritans, to fast. They did it to purify the body and make it more fit to hear the voice of God but he did it rigorously, as an act of penance, until his legs trembled and buckled under him from weakness. He kept vigils as well, staying awake night after night, sometimes sitting in utter darkness and sometimes with a glimmering lamp. Sometimes he would stare at his face in a mirror, using the strongest light he had.

Here was introspection twisted by torment and without any value as a cure. In these extended vigils his brain often reeled and visions seemed to flit before him. Sometimes he saw a herd of diabolic shapes that grinned and mocked him, and called him to come away with them and at other times he would see a band of shining but sorrow-laden angels that vanished as they rose. He saw the dead friends of his youth, his white-bearded father with a saintly frown, his mother turning her face away as she passed by. That was a ghost of a mother—the thinnest fantasy of a mother—I think she would still have thrown a pitying glance towards her son! And he would see Hester Prynne gliding through his visions, leading little Pearl along. In her scarlet gown she would point her forefinger first at the scarlet letter on her own and then at the clergyman's chest.

Though they gave him added pain none of these visions ever quite deluded him. At any moment, by an effort of his will he always knew where he was and what they were. Over there he could see and recognize a table of carved oak, or a big, square, leather-bound and brazen-clasped volume of theology so he knew where he was and that they were substantial. But for all that, in one sense his visions and fantasies were the truest and most substantial things the poor minister now dealt with. It's the unspeakable misery of a life as false as his that it steals the heart and substance out of whatever realities there are around it; realities that were meant by Heaven to be the spirit's joy and nourishment. To the untrue man the whole universe is false—it is vague and unreal—it shrinks to nothing within his grasp.

And he himself becomes a shadow because he unceasingly presents himself in a false light. The man no longer exists—only a shadow remains. The only truth that continued to give young Dimmesdale an authentic existence on this earth was the anguish in his inmost soul because that was real and so was the way it showed itself. Smiles were impossible and the happy face if he had had the power to show one would have had no man behind it. There was no such man; a smiling man didn't exist.

On one of those ugly visionary nights the minister jumped from his chair. A new thought had struck him. He might gain a moment's peace through it. Dressing himself with as much care as if it had been going to public worship he stole softly down the staircase, undid the door, and went out into the night.

12

The Minister's Vigil

He was walking as if he was dreaming but he might actually have been in some sort of trance; in any case, he finally came to where he wanted to be. It was the place where Hester Prynne had lived through her first hours of public shame and disgrace. It was the same platform or scaffold, black and weather-beaten with the storm or sunshine of seven long years. It was foot-worn too because a host of culprits had climbed those steps and stood there shamed beneath the balcony of the meeting-house. He climbed the awful steps.

It was a chilly night in early May and visibility was poor. An unbroken mass of moving cloud covered the whole expanse of sky all the way to the horizon. If the multitude that watched Hester Prynne's agony and punishment were watching now they wouldn't have been able to recognize the face above the platform; they would hardly have made out the outline of a human shape in the dark gray of the midnight. As it was, the town was dead in sleep so he was in no danger of being discovered. The only risk he was taking was that the dank and chill night air would creep into his feeble frame and rob the expectant assembly of tomorrow's prayer and sermon. No eye would see him—except one! It was that tireless, rarely-sleeping eye that had seen him in his little private room secretly and all alone beating himself with the bloody scourge. Surely that beating should have been enough. If so, why had he made his way in the dead of night to this God-forsaken spot? Was it no more than a mock repentance? Yes, it was certainly mockery, but it was an anguished and desperate soul trifling with itself! A mockery at which angels must have blushed and wept while demonic fiends rejoiced with jeering laughter! He had been driven there by that creature Remorse who unceasingly drove him here and there and everywhere, even to the edge of the abyss of full confession and disclosure. But then the sister of Remorse who went wherever Remorse went pulled him back with a grip he couldn't resist. Her name was Cowardice. Poor, miserable man! What lunacy it was for someone with a nature as brittle and sensitive as his to involve himself with crime! Crime should be reserved for those with nerves of iron, who have their choice either to endure it with patience, or, if it pressed too hard to exert their fierce and savage strength for a good purpose and fling it off in an open confession! This feeble and most sensitive soul could do neither and yet he did both in secret.

Mortally afraid of the pain of exposure yet heaping the kind of pain on his soul and body that heroes would collapse under. Here was a puny little human caught between overwhelming forces, torn apart between a heaven-defying guilt and a repentance he needed to repent of and couldn't.

And so, while standing on the scaffold in this awful show of atonement that didn't atone and left him still feeling forsaken, Dimmesdale was overcome with a great horror of mind. He felt as if the universe were staring at a scarlet token on his naked chest, right over his heart. In point of fact, on that spot, that very place, pain had been gnawing on him for a long time with a poisonous tooth. Unable to keep himself from it but without any intention of doing it he heard himself shriek into the night. It was a mad shriek that went on rippling into the dark and echoed back off the walls of buildings and houses in the area, even muttering back from the hills in the distance. A company of drunk demons that gathered near the awful scaffold must have heard so much misery and terror in the sound that they had made a plaything of it and were kicking it back and forward in the night as children do with a tin can.

"It's done!" muttered the minister, covering his face with his hands.

"The whole town will awake and hurry out, and find me here!" But it wasn't to be; his torment was to go on longer. The shriek might not have been as loud as it sounded to his own startled ears but be that as it may, the town didn't awake. If one or two did awake, in their drowsy state they would have interpreted it in one of a number of ways so the frightened clergyman uncovered his eyes and looked around him. In the distance, at one window of Governor

Bellingham's mansion in the next street, he was able to make out the figure of the old magistrate himself with a lamp in his hand. He looked like a ghost from the graveyard that wondered what the noise was all about. He had obviously heard the cry and it had startled him. At another window his sister, old Mistress Hibbins, held her lamp and though it was distant her sour and discontented face was clearly visible. She shoved her head out of the window and anxiously looked up and there was no doubt that the venerable witch-woman had heard the sound. Witch that she was she was sure she knew it was some of her friends. The magistrate, after peering into the darkness and seeing nothing went back to bed.

He was calmer now. But in a moment or two he saw a little glimmering light coming nearer. It was a long way off at first but as it came closer it threw a gleam on a post here and a garden fence there, a latticed window-pane and a pump with its full trough of water, even an iron knocker and a rough log for the door-step. All this the watching minister noted even though he was hypnotized. Like a rodent facing a snake, unable to move, he saw the light come nearer and he was sure that his fate was sealed and his doom was at hand.

In a moment or two the gleam of the lantern would expose him and in a few moments more his long-hidden secret would be known to the world; panic filled him but he couldn't hide. As the light drew nearer, he saw his professional father and valued friend—the Reverend Mr. Wilson, who had been praying at the deathbed of Governor Winthrop who had moved from earth to heaven within that very hour. Wilson looked as if the departed Governor had left him an abundance of glory or that he himself had caught the distant shine of the celestial city as he watched the triumphant pilgrim pass inside its gates. The glimmer of this lamp suggested all that foolishness to Mr. Dimmesdale, who smiled—no, almost laughed at them—and then wondered if he wasn't already mad.

As the Reverend Mr. Wilson passed beside the scaffold muffled with a cloak against the damp and chilly night Dimmesdale could hardly keep himself from speaking.

"A good evening to you, venerable Father Wilson. Come up here if you would and pass a pleasant hour with me!" Good Heavens! Had he actually spoken? For one instant he believed he had, but he spoke only in his imagination. The old preacher continued his homeward way, paying careful attention to the muddy road and never once glancing toward the platform of shame and pain. It was only when the light of the lantern had faded right away that the minister realized that the last few moments had been a crisis of terrible anxiety. He found himself close to fainting.

But the fears and fantasies generated by his guilt weren't finished, as all that are burdened by hidden guilt would know from experience.

He felt his limbs growing numb with the chilliness of the night and he began to doubt seriously whether he would be able to get down the steps of the scaffold. He was sure the morning would come and the neighborhood would awake to find him there. The earliest riser, in the dim half-light would make out the vaguely defined figure up there, and half-alarmed and half-curious he would call out his neighbors. The word would fly from one house to another and before long the trickle would become a stream and the stream a river and the river an ocean of faces—aghast and staring at him. Old Governor Bellingham would come, grim and severe; saintly Father Wilson would be there too with the elders and deacons of Dimmesdale's church. The young worshipful virgins who so idolized their minister and had made a shrine for him in their tender hearts would arrive. All the people in his world would come stumbling from their houses to be amazed and horrified by the spectacle on the scaffold. And who would they see there but the Reverend Arthur Dimmesdale, frozen near to death, overwhelmed with shame and finally exposed for the lying hypocrite that he was.

Carried away by the terror and the awful absurdity of this picture the minister burst into a great peal of laughter. Utterly unexpected—for how could he have expected it—a light and childish laugh that he recognized as Pearl's followed his.

"Pearl! Oh Pearl!" he shouted after a moment's pause. Then, suppressing his voice he called, "Hester! Hester Prynne! Are you there?"

"I'm here," she replied with some surprise in her tone as she approached the minister. "Pearl and I are here."

"Where have you come from, Hester?" asked the minister. "What sent you here?"

"I've been at Governor Winthrop's deathbed. They asked me to make him a robe for the funeral and I was on my way home." "Come up here, Hester, you and Pearl," the trembling man said.

"You have both been here before but you were alone and I should have been with you. Come up here again and all three of us will stand together."

She silently climbed the steps and stood on the platform, holding the little girl by the hand. The minister felt for the child's other hand, found it and took it. The moment that he did it he felt a tumultuous rush of new life pouring like a torrent into his heart and pulsating through all his veins, as if the mother and the child were transfusing their vital warmth into his fading body.

"Minister!" whispered little Pearl.

"Yes, child?"

"Will you stand here with mother and me tomorrow at noon?"

"No, Pearl," he said. The feeling of new life was inspiring but it couldn't be leaned on. The newly found courage was as passing as the mist that's burned away as soon as the sun shows itself over the rim of the world. With the child's pointed question all the dread of public exposure had returned in a rush and he found himself whimpering again, amazed that he thought only a moment ago that he could do it.

"No, my child. I will indeed stand with you and your mother one other day, but not to-morrow."

She laughed and attempted to pull her hand away but the minister held it tight.

"Just a moment longer, child!" he said.

"But will you promise," Pearl persisted, "to take my hand and my mother's hand tomorrow at noon?"

"Not then, Pearl," said the minister, "but another time."

"And what other time?" she prodded.

"At the great judgment day," whispered the minister; "your mother and you and I must stand together. But not in this world!" Pearl laughed again.

But before Dimmesdale had done speaking a meteorite lit up the sky and the light, caught beneath the clouds as if it were in a bowl,

133

revealed the whole street with the brightness of noon. In the awesome light and in such an unnatural setting the world was bathed in a strange newness. The familiar no longer seemed the same and details as small and as insignificant as wheel tracks were invested with some moral meaning. But what were the sharpened shadows and the jutting roofs and gable peaks telling? And there in the light that could almost be felt stood the minister with his hand over his heart and Hester Prynne with the embroidered letter glimmering and Pearl, herself a living symbol and connecting link between those two.

They stood in the strange noon of that weird and solemn splendor as if it were the light that revealed all secrets and the daybreak that would unite all who belong to one another.

There was witchcraft in the girl's eyes and in her face as she glanced up at the minister. She wore that cunning smile that was more of a smirk or a leer that suggested things people don't wish to put into words or even to think about. She withdrew her hand from Mr. Dimmesdale's and pointed across the street but he clutched his chest and kept looking at the sky.

Nothing was more common, in those days, than to interpret all meteoric appearances and other unusual phenomena as revelations from a supernatural source. So a blazing spear, a sword of flame, a bow, or a sheaf of arrows seen in the midnight sky prefigured Indian warfare. Pestilence was known to be on the way when crimson light was seen. I doubt if any marked event good or evil ever befell New England, from its settlement down to revolutionary times, that wasn't foretold by some spectacle of nature. Often the signs were seen by multitudes but more often its credibility rested on the testimony of some lonely eyewitness who saw the wonder or imagined he did, and later embellished it. Still, the notion is majestic. Heaven itself is a fitting scroll for Providence to write these awesome signs on when it reveals the destiny of a nation. The conviction was a favorite one with our forefathers, especially in light of the new beginning of their infant commonwealth. God was making it clear that he was truly interested in their welfare and expressed it in blessing as well as strictness. But what are we to say when an individual discovers a revelation that is addressed to him alone on the same vast page? There's surely a colossal egotism involved in such a case. It can only be the symptom of a highly disordered mental state, experienced by a man too self-conscious as a result of long and intense pain. Imagine a solitary human thinking that the heavens themselves should be no more than a writing pad to plot the course of his soul's history and fate. So I hold that when the minister looked up to heaven and saw an immense letter A marked out in lines of dull red light it was another symptom of his diseased mind. No doubt some other poor soul with a heart burdened with guilt would have seen something other than the letter A.

But just as he had turned his eyes skyward to look in horror he got a fleeting glimpse of something nearer home. The horror he thought he saw in the sky was matched by a horror Pearl saw across the street and pointed at. It was old Chillingworth. He too was bathed in that unearthly light and it might well be that in the dusk the skilled man thought he didn't need to hide the malevolence with which he looked on his victim. In the strange light he would have passed for the Devil himself. There he stood with a smile that was a scowl, claiming his own.

"Who is that man, Hester?" gasped Mr. Dimmesdale, overcome with terror. "I shiver at him! Do you know him? I hate him, Hester!" She remained silent. She had sworn.

"I tell you, my soul shivers at him!" hissed the minister again. "Who is he? Who is he? Can you do nothing for me? I have a nameless dread of that man!"

"Minister," said the child, "I can tell you who he is!"

"Quickly, then, child!" said the minister, bending his ear close to her lips. "Quickly, and as low as you can whisper." She mumbled noises into his ear that sounded something like human language but it was only the childish gibberish that children amuse themselves with. At any rate, if it involved any secret information about the doctor it was in a language the educated clergyman didn't recognize and it only increased his confusion and fear. The eerie child laughed out loud.

"Do you mock me now?" said the minister.

"You were not brave!—you were not true!" she said. "You wouldn't promise to take my hand and my mother's hand tomorrow at noon!"

Then another voice pretending surprise chimed in. "Worthy sir!" It was the physician, who had now advanced to the foot of the platform—"Why, it's pious Master Dimmesdale! Can this really be you? Well, well, indeed! We men of study, with heads filled with our books need to be looked after with great care! We dream in our waking moments and walk in our sleep. Come, my dear friend, please, let me take you home!"

"How did you know I was here?" asked the minister, almost afraid to ask.

"Honestly, and in good faith," Chillingworth lied, "I didn't know. I had spent the better part of the night at the bedside of the Governor Winthrop doing the little I could to give him ease, though I knew he was going home to a better world. Then I was on my way to my home when this light shone out. Come with me, I beg you, Reverend sir, or you'll not be able to do your Sabbath duty tomorrow." And as he spoke he reached reassuringly for the minister. "Your trouble is that you are too devoted, my dear friend. Much study is a weariness to the flesh—isn't that what the Good Book says? You see now how they trouble the brain—these books! You should study less, good sir, and take a little pastime or these night whimsies will grow on you."

All the while he spoke in soothing tones he was stretching out his arm to help the poor soul. The skillful man's pretence was working. Perhaps he had seen nothing and heard nothing. Perhaps, the minister thought to himself, the doctor really did think he had walked in his sleep.

"I will go home with you," said Mr. Dimmesdale.

With a chill despondency, like one awakening, all nerveless, from an ugly dream, he allowed the doctor to lead him away, weary and weak beyond measure.

But the next day, however astonishing it sounds, he preached a sermon that was held to be the richest and most powerful that had ever proceeded from his lips. It was filled with heaven's influence and many souls were brought to the truth by the power of that sermon and they vowed to cherish a holy gratitude towards Mr.

Dimmesdale throughout eternity. But as he came down the pulpit steps, the gray-bearded sexton met him, holding up a black glove that the minister recognized as his own.

"Someone found it," said the sexton, "this morning on the scaffold where evil-doers are set up to public shame. No doubt Satan dropped it there, intending a scurrilous joke against you. But he was as blind and foolish as ever and always is. A pure hand needs no glove to cover it!"

"Thank you, my good friend," the minister said gravely, but startled at heart. He was so confused that he had almost brought himself to believe the events of the past night were dreams or hallucinations.

"Yes, it seems to be my glove, all right!"

"And, since Satan saw fit to steal it, your reverence needs to handle him without gloves from now on," remarked the old sexton, grimly smiling. "But did your reverence hear of the sign that was seen last night? A great red letter in the sky—the letter A, which we interpret to stand for Angel. For, our good Governor Winthrop was made an angel last night and no doubt heaven saw fit to take some notice of it!"

"No," answered the minister; "I had not heard of it."

13

Another view of Hester

Seeing Mr. Dimmesdale that night at the scaffold shocked Hester. She could hardly believe what the clergyman had been reduced to. He was a nervous wreck, his moral force was gone and what was left was groveling weakness; a child had more strength and fortitude. All that was true even though his intellect seemed at least as strong as ever and maybe even more focused. She had noted that disease sometimes sharpened the perception of certain people. With her intimate and privileged knowledge she was sure that besides the legitimate action of his own conscience, some terrible power was operating against the minister, destroying his health and peace of mind.

Knowing what this fallen man had once been, her whole soul was moved by the way he had asked for help against his enemy.

Shuddering with terror he had appealed to her—an outcast woman—against an enemy he was powerless against. She decided that he had a right to all the help she could give him but she was so unsure of herself; how exactly could she help and where exactly did her responsibility lie since her link with this man was a criminal one? This she knew, all links to society were made of silk or satin, fabric and flowers but the links to this man were made of iron and she couldn't break them. But she was no longer the same Hester.

Seven years had passed and major changes had taken place in and for her. The townspeople had now become accustomed to seeing Pearl and her mother with the glittering scarlet letter on her dress. The pair was no longer gaped at and since she served the colony well and interfered with no one she and her daughter were generally accepted. It's to the credit of human nature that while there are notable exceptions, it loves more readily than it hates. A gradual and quiet process can transform even bitter hatred to love, or at least to tolerance and kindness, providing the original feeling of hostility isn't fed by continuous irritations. In this case, Hester was neither an irritation nor a continued offence. She never battled with the public, but submitted uncomplainingly to its worst behavior toward her; she asked no apology for the pain they subjected her to and she didn't seek its pity. Then there was the blameless purity of her life during all these years; that weighed heavily in her favor. With nothing now to lose in the sight of society and with no hope, and apparently no wish to gain anything, her regard for virtue was taken as genuine, the prodigal truly had come home.

There was this too: the people saw that she was very generous.

She was a hard-worker and provided for all that she and Pearl needed. It would have been sheer nonsense to suggest she had gathered a lot of money but it was crystal clear that when someone was in need she helped. Nor was she in search of praise for her good works because it was well known that more than once what she got in return for the food or clothes she regularly provided was insult and jibes. Some poor souls in need of clothes hadn't the sense to accept in gratitude what she did for them! This woman that could make grand robes for aristocrats and rulers troubled herself to provide for the thankless and rude. And when infections stalked the colony and raged through sorrowing and fear-filled homes and the town reeled, there she was shoulder to shoulder not just with the commoners but with the ladies of society. She didn't come as a guest but as someone that belonged, as if their pain and suffering gave her the right to be one with her fellow-humans. In all places of trouble and need or loneliness and despair the embroidered letter gleamed with—how do you explain it?—some added comfort. Under other circumstances it was the token of sin but in the presence of disease and loss it was the warm comforting light of the sick room. Those that were dying often asked for her as well as a minister and her very presence would speak and show them where to put their feet on their uncertain journey. In such emergencies she showed herself warm and rich—a wellspring of human tenderness, unfailing in every real demand and, or so it seemed, boundless in energy. She was self-ordained a Sister of Mercy. Well, perhaps it would be more accurate to say the world's heavy hand had so ordained her though neither she nor the world ever dreamed this would be the end result. The letter became the symbol of her calling. Such helpfulness was found in her—so much power to do and power to sympathize—that many people refused to interpret the scarlet A by its original significance and said it meant Able! But for all this change, the seven years hadn't changed her. She didn't feel free and she hadn't become gay and bright. She didn't gossip freely with the women or join the little groups for harmless chatter, and much less did she hang around to receive the thanks of a grateful community—presuming it to be there and that they wanted to offer it. No, if she met them in the street she never raised her head to receive their greeting but if they were determined to speak to her she would lay her finger on the scarlet letter and move on. It might have been pride, of course, or a subtle way of rejecting the society that had so decisively rejected her but it might just as easily have been humility. It was so like humility that it had all the softening influence that that virtue has on the respectable public mind. The public is a tyrant in its temper! It's capable of denying common justice when it is demanded too strenuously as a right but just as surely, it frequently awards more than cold justice when the appeal is made to the tyrant's generosity—and doesn't it love to have it that way? Interpreting Hester Prynne's behavior and attitude as an appeal to its better nature society tended to show its former victim more warmth and friendliness than she cared to receive, and certainly more than she thought she deserved The common people were quicker to acknowledge the influence of Hester's goodness than the leaders and the learned men of the community. The prejudices of the leaders and the learned were fortified by an iron framework of reasoning so it was harder for them to get rid of them. But day by day their sour and rigid wrinkles were relaxing into something that might almost be mistaken for benevolence. That's how it is with men of rank whose eminenence makes them guardians of the public morals. Individuals in private life had quite forgiven Hester Prynne for her weakness. No, more than that, they had begun to look on the scarlet letter as the token not of her sin but of her many good deeds since then.

"Do you see that woman with the embroidered badge?" they would say to strangers. "It's our Hester—the town's own Hester—she's so kind to the poor, so helpful to the sick and so comforting to the afflicted!" But true to the worst moments in us they would feel the need to whisper to them the black scandal of bygone years. Nevertheless, in the eyes of the very men who whispered the story—and they always found some "good reason" to insist it must be told—the scarlet letter had the effect of the cross on a nun's garment. It gave Hester a kind of sacredness that allowed her to walk securely without fear. If she had fallen among thieves it would have kept her safe. It was reported, and many believed it, that an Indian shot an arrow at her and that it struck the symbol and fell harmless to the ground.

But while it's true that the seven years hadn't changed her in the sense that she still felt unworthy of the free company of good people, they had certainly changed her in other ways. All that was light and bright and graceful in her character had been withered by this red-hot brand and had long ago fallen away. She was now almost a harsh outline of her former self and if she had had friends or companions that hadn't seen her in a long time the change would have been enough to shock them. Even her appearance was affected. Part of it was due to the deliberate dullness of her clothes and part to the loss of passion and gaiety in her manners. She hid her rich and luxuriant hair under a cap or cut off at times so that not a shining curl of it ever once gushed into the sunshine. All these things conspired to transform her appearance but there was something else in addition to all of these. There was no longer anything in Hester's face for love to dwell on; there was nothing about her form or figure that passion would ever dream of holding in its embrace; there was noting about her now that would generate affection or romance. Something had vanished from her that a woman must have to remain womanly. That frequently happens when a woman has encountered and lived through an experience of peculiar severity. If she's all tenderness she'll die. If she survives, the tenderness will either be crushed out of her or so deeply suppressed that it can never show itself again.

Well...perhaps, but a woman that has ceased to be truly womanly might at any moment become that way again if there's magic enough in a touch to effect the transformation. We'll see whether Hester Prynne was ever afterwards so touched and so transfigured.

A number of things had drained Hester of passion and feeling and turned her into something resembling cold marble, but none more surely than the isolation she had endured. Standing alone in the world, independent of society and with Pearl to guide and protect, had obviously robbed her of human fellowship and that alone robbed her of much that she needed. Not only had she been robbed of social communion in actual fact, she was robbed of any hope of retrieving it, even if she had wanted to do that. So she changed and turned away from all avenues of mutual social warming. But the world had changed as well. The individual was discovered one more time and the human intellect set free had begun to range more widely than it had done for many centuries. Men of the sword had overthrown nobles and kings and men bolder than these had overthrown and rearranged the whole system of ancient prejudice and principle.

Hester Prynne drank of this spirit and allowed her mind to reflect in ways that if the fathers in the New World had known it they would have held her guilty of a crime worse than adultery. In her lonesome cottage by the seashore she thought things that no other home in New England entertained.

It's remarkable but not at all rare that people that speculate most boldly are often content to conform to the external regulations of society. The thought is enough for them and they don't feel the need to put it into social action. That's how it seemed to be with Hester but if Pearl had never come into her life things might have been altogether different. Who knows, she could well have come down to us in history hand in hand with Ann Hutchinson as the founder of a religious sect, or a prophetess. She might, and most probably would, have suffered death from the stern tribunals of the period for attempting to undermine the foundations of the Puritan establishment.

But the child kept her from all this because Pearl had to be raised to enable her to make her way through life in a world very different from the one that whirled around in her mother's head. Everything in the hostile world was against the child so Hester didn't need to make it harder on her by raising her in religious rebellion. Even the child's own nature was against the child, there was that strange element in her that suggested there was something awry in her birth—was her mother's lawless passion somehow poured into her? Repeatedly Hester asked herself in bitterness of heart and soul whether Pearl's birth was a good thing.

She raised dark questions about womanhood. Was existence worth accepting even for the happiest among them? She had long ago made up her mind about her own existence and had decided that the answer *no* was beyond debate. She believed that for a woman, if life were to be worth living the whole fabric of society would have to be torn down and rebuilt. A woman's nature would have to be redefined by allowing her to shake off the long established roles assigned to her and allowing her to be shaped by new habits rather than the hereditary ones with which she'd been saddled. Without such radical changes women would never know fairness and freedom in society and she knew that that would never happen—it was a pipe dream. But even assuming all the initial difficulties were removed, a woman wouldn't be able to take advantage of the reforms until she herself changed, and if she did she might discover that the heart of her heart had evaporated. A woman never overcomes these problems by philosophy. If they are to be solved it is only in one way.

If her heart takes the lead the problems vanish. That is why Hester Prynne, whose heart had lost its regular and healthy throb, wandered without a clue in the dark tunnels of her mind. At times a terrifying thought came, almost taking possession of her soul: would it not be better to send Pearl to Heaven at once? The scarlet letter hadn't done what it was meant to do. But then again, maybe it had.

But now that awful night at the scaffold with the Reverend Mr. Dimmesdale had given her a new theme to reflect on and offered her something worth fighting and sacrificing for. She had seen the intense misery the minister struggled against, or, maybe it was more accurate to say she had seen the awful misery he had ceased to struggle against. She saw him on the edge of lunacy, if he had not already stepped across it. It was plain to see that whatever power the sting of secret remorse had to hurt him, that a deadlier venom was being injected into him by the hand that pretended to offer relief. And since the doctor was trusted he could work in perfect security, having all the time in the world to perfect and fine-tune his methods and he had countless opportunities to tamper with the delicate springs of Mr. Dimmesdale's nature. Hester blamed herself for not being truthful, courageous and loyal. She had allowed the minister to be put at risk where so much evil was to be expected and nothing good could be hoped for. She told herself that it was that the only way of keeping him from a blacker ruin than the one that had fallen on her was to agree to Chillingworth's oath of silence; she now knew she had made the wrong choice. She now determined to do whatever she needed to do to right the wrong as far as she was able.

Strengthened by years of hard and solemn trial she no longer felt inadequate to cope with Roger Chillingworth. She had been no match for him that night, when crushed by sin and half-maddened by the shame that was still new to her but he would meet a different woman the next time because she had risen higher. The old man on the other hand had brought himself down to her sinful level by the cruel and malignant revenge he had stooped to take. She was stronger than the shrewd man now.

She didn't have to wait long for the confrontation. One afternoon when she was walking with Pearl in a part of the peninsula not much used she saw the old physician with a basket on one arm and a staff in the other hand searching for roots and herbs to make his medicine.

The scene was set and the actors were in place.

14

Hester and the Physician

She sent Pearl down to the margin of the water to play and away she flew like a bird and found an orphaned pool and dialogued with the face that looked out at her. Without a friend to play with it all made perfect and reasonable nonsense to Pearl but the figure in the pool wouldn't leave the pool.

Meanwhile it wasn't playful nonsense the mother had in mind when she approached the physician.

"I want a word with you," she said, "about something that concerns us both very much."

"Aha! so Mistress Hester has a word for old Roger Chillingworth, does she?" raising himself from his stooping posture. "That would please me no end! Why, mistress, everywhere I go I hear grand reports about you! Only yesterday evening a magistrate, a wise and

149

godly man, was going on and on about, Mistress Hester, and he whispered to me that the council is so impressed with her that they were wondering if it wasn't time that that scarlet letter be removed from her. They no longer see you as a threat to the common good and on my life, Hester, I begged the worshipful magistrate to have it done right away."

"The removal of the badge has nothing to do with the pleasure of the magistrates," she replied calmly but decisively—she mustn't accept kind remarks from him because it would only make it harder to speak plainly. "If I were worthy to be done with it, it would drop off by itself or come to mean something other than it has meant."

"No? Well then, wear it if it suits you better. A woman should follow her own fancy about the way she dresses herself. The letter is wonderfully embroidered and looks very well on you!"

While they spoke Hester had been looking steadily at the old man and was shocked as well as wonder-smitten to see what a change had come over him within the past seven years. It wasn't so much that he had grown older for though the traces of advancing life were visible he bore his age well and he seemed to retain a wiry vigor and alertness. But he used to have "intellectual and studious man," written all over him, he had been calm and quiet, and that was how she best remembered him. But that look had altogether vanished and his appearance and manner now struck her as feverish, eager, searching, almost fierce and yet...suppressed and guarded. It seemed to be his wish and purpose to mask this expression with a smile but the smile let him down because it flickered across his face so falsely that a perceptive viewer could see his moral deviance all the better for it. And frequently, without warning, a sort of glaring redness shone out of his eyes as if the old man's soul were on fire and was smoldering and smoking down inside, until by some whiff of passion it was blown into a momentary flame. When that happened he would repress it as quickly as possible and then try to look as if nothing of the kind had happened; but there it was.

In a word, old Roger Chillingworth was a striking illustration of and evidence for man's capacity to become satanic. This miserable and lost man had worked such a transformation by devoting himself, in the name of learning, for seven years to the constant analysis of a tortured heart. There is some knowledge we should not want to gain.

It is vile labor and the work of a degenerate to seek to know how much torment a human can endure before disintegrating. It doesn't matter that it can be written in a medical journal that might somehow be useful to some future generation. What was worse, he gloated in pleasure as he watched the sufferer writhe while he tested his skill to see how well he could make the victim writhe.

Feelings of guilt burned into Hester because here, she thought, was another ruin for which she was responsible.

"What do you see in my face," he asked, "that makes you look at it so earnestly?"

"Something that would make me weep if there were any tears bitter enough for it," she said. "But let it pass! It's that other miserable man that I want to speak about."

"And what of him?" cried Chillingworth, eagerly, as if he loved the topic and was glad of an opportunity to discuss it with the only person he could confide in.

"The truth of the matter is, Mistress Hester, I have been thinking about that very gentleman. So let's have an open and frank discussion about him."

"We last spoke together about seven years ago that was neither open nor frank," she began, "and it pleased you to extort a promise of secrecy about our former relationship. And because the life and good name of that man were in your hands I thought I had no choice except to be silent since you insisted on that. But I suspected then that something sinister was in your mind so it was with a nagging uncertainty I agreed. I cared nothing for others but I felt a profound debt toward him and something whispered in me that I was betraying him by pledging myself to keep your counsel. Since that day no man is so near to him as you. You follow his every footstep as though you were his very shadow, you're beside him, sleeping and waking. You search his thoughts. You burrow and fester in his heart! You grip his heart like a vise and you kill him every day even while you keep him alive so that he can die again; and still he hasn't seen through you. In letting this go on I've been false to the only man I had the power to be true to!"

"What choice had you?" asked misshapen Chillingworth. "I had only to point my finger at this man and they would have hurled him from his pulpit into a pit and from there perhaps to swinging and creaking in the breeze!"

"It would have been better if that had happened," she said.

"What evil have I done the man?" he asked in mock surprise, "I tell you, Hester Prynne, the richest fee that any doctor would have earned from any monarch couldn't have bought the kind of care I have wasted on this miserable priest! If it hadn't been for me his life would have burned away in torment within two years after he committed his crime. For, Hester, his spirit lacked the strength that could have borne up as yours has done beneath a burden like your scarlet letter. Oh, I could reveal a goodly secret! But enough! What skill and devotion can do, I have exhausted on him. That he still breathes and creeps about on earth is owing all to me!"

"Better he had died at once!" she spat out.

"Yes, you're right there, woman!" he snarled, letting the lurid fire of his heart blaze out before her eyes. "It would have been better for him if he had died at once! Never did mortal suffer what this man has suffered. And all, all, before the ecstatic eyes of his worst enemy!" His eyes were burning and shining now as he got into an evil rhythm. "He has been conscious of me. He has felt an influence settling down on him like a feeding parasite. He knew, by some spiritual sense—for the Creator never made another being so sensitive as this one—he knew it was no friendly hand that was pulling at his heartstrings and he knew that a malevolent eye was burning into him, looking only for evil and finding it." Triumph and delight now rang in his voice. "But he never dreamed that the eye and hand were mine! With the superstition common to his brotherhood he thought he had been given over to a fiend to be tortured with frightful dreams and desperate thoughts. He babbles on about the sting of remorse and despair of pardon being a foretaste of what awaits him beyond the grave. But it was the constant shadow of my presence, it was the nearer than nearness of the man he had most vilely wronged, and who exists only to extract revenge by this slow poison! He thought it was a demon, and you understand, he wasn't wrong for there is a fiend at his elbow! A mortal man that once had a human heart has become a demon for no other purpose than to torment him."

As he spoke these words the obsessed doctor lifted his hands with a look of horror as if he had just seen some hideous shape in a mirror taking his place. It was one of those rare moments, if a man is fortunate, when his true moral character is faithfully and vividly and frighteningly made bare before him. Chillingworth had just seen himself for the first time. It could have been a redeeming moment.

"Have you not tortured him enough?" said Hester, taking full notice of the old man's look. "Has he not by now paid you in full?"

The redeeming moment vanished. "No, no! He has only increased the debt!" hissed the physician, and then began to calm down before finally subsiding into gloom.

"Do you remember me, Hester, as I was nine years ago? Even then I was in the late autumn of my days. But all my life had been made up of earnest, studious, thoughtful, quiet years, bestowed faithfully for the increase of my own knowledge. I grant that I sought my own development but I meant also to be a benefit to humanity. No life had been more peaceful and innocent than mine and I had done much good. Do you remember me? Was I not— though you might have thought me cold—was I not nevertheless a man that was thoughtful for others, craving little for himself but, just the same, kind, true and constant, if not warm in affection? Was I not all this?"

"All this, and more," she confessed.

"And what am I now?" he demanded, looking into her face, letting her reflect on the sin that now possessed him. "I have already told you what I am—a monstrous evil! And who made me like this?"

154

"You did," cried Hester, shuddering. "You did it to yourself. And if it was him that hurt you it was me too, me no less than him. Why have you not avenged yourself on me?"

"I have left you to the scarlet letter," replied Roger Chillingworth. "If that has not been enough I can do no more!" He laid his finger on it with a smile.

"It accomplished all you could have wanted," she assured him.

"I judged no less," said the physician. "And now what do you want to say to me about this man?"

"I'm going to tell him," answered Hester, firmly. "He has a right to know who you really are! I don't know what the result will be when I tell him but that I have kept this secret from him and it has been the torment and ruin of him. I owe him a debt and I will pay it! I'm aware that I have his reputation, career, his life and maybe even his death in my hands. But I know the truth now; it's no advantage to him to live this way any longer. I won't beg you for mercy for him. Do with him as you see fit. There's no good for him or me and there's no good for you. There's no good even for the child. Whichever path we take there's no way out of this dismal maze."

"Woman, I could nearly pity you," he said, unable to restrain a thrill of admiration at the quality that was almost majesty in the despair she expressed. "You were gifted with wondrous gifts. Perhaps if you had met earlier with a better love than mine this evil would never have been. I do pity you for all the good that has been wasted in your nature."

"And I you," answered Hester, "for the hatred that has transformed a wise and just man into a vindictive wretch! Will you not make an attempt to purge it out of you and become human

155

again? If not for his sake then doubly for your own! Forgive him and leave his further punishment to the Power that claims it! I said a moment ago that there could be no good for any of us but that isn't true. There might be good for you and you alone since thou have been deeply wronged and have the chance to pardon. Don't give up that only privilege! It's such a priceless benefit. Forgive him."

"Peace, Hester—peace!" replied the old man, with gloomy sternness, "It's not given to me to pardon. I have no such power. My old faith that I have long ignored explains all that we do and all we suffer. Your first step downward planted the germ of evil but from that moment on it has all been a dark necessity. You two that have wronged me are not sinful, that's simply babble and neither am I a fiend that has taken over a demon's work. It's our fate. Let the black flower blossom as it may! Now, go your way and deal with the man however you see fit."

He waved her away with his hand; waved away a precious opportunity and went back to gathering herbs.

15

Hester and Pearl Again

Hester watched Chillingworth limp off stooped and twisted and as she watched, it seemed to her that he was the epitome of evil. A corrupt and corrupting soul that polluted everything he came in contact with whether he touched it with his mind or his hands. Did the sun that shines everywhere really shine on him? Was it just her imagination when she thought that even as he moved in the sunlight an aura of shadow enveloped him? In her heart she knew she only projected her feelings and fears and trembling sense of his unholy inner darkness on to him, but she half expected the ground to open up and swallow him and leave a barren and blasted spot. Maybe it was that she wished it would and that later, to mark the spot, it would send up some poisonous shrubs and fungus. She looked and mused long enough and finally murmured bitterly to herself,

"Whether it's sin or not, I hate the man!" She reproached herself for the sentiment but couldn't overcome or lessen it because she had begun to despise even herself for ever having had anything to do with him. She reflected on those early days in a distant land when he would come from his study in the evening and sit down at the fire and bask in the warmth of his young wife's smile. He said it took the chill off his scholar's heart. What grieved her now was the fact that she had once thought these to be happy moments whereas now, looked at in light of her dismal existence, she classed them among her ugliest memories. It amazed her that she could ever have agreed to marry him! What possessed her? She raged against herself that the crime most to be repented of was that she had ever endured and returned the lukewarm grasp of his hand.

It disgusted her that she had allowed her smile and eyes to mingle and melt into his own. And she was sure that no offence committed against him was ever as foul as the one he had committed against her. He knew she was young and foolish when he met her and he knew that she could never be happy with him but he went ahead and bound her to him. All that he did, knowing he was doing it at her expense and that he was doing it to satisfy his own cold craving. If Dimmesdale had cheapened Chillingworth by provoking bitterness, malice and misery in him by sinning against him, how great a crime had Chillingworth committed against Hester? "Yes, I hate him!" repeated Hester more bitterly than before. "He betrayed me! He has done worse to me than I did him!" And so the evil continued to ripple outward in widening circles as sinners mutually added ruin to ruin and loss to loss.

Let men tremble to win the hand of a woman unless they win along with it the utmost passion of her heart, for it might end in misery when some touch more thrilling than their own wakens all her sensibilities.

It happened to Roger Chillingworth, who was reproached for the marble image of happiness that he imposed on Hester as a substitute for the warm reality.

But Hester had had long enough to put this injustice out of her mind. What did it say about her that she still mulled it over with such intensity? That seven long years under the torture of the scarlet letter, inflicted so much misery but produced no repentance? The emotion of those brief moments, while she stood gazing after the crooked figure, threw a dark light on Hester's state of mind, revealing much that she might not otherwise have acknowledged to herself. When he had vanished from sight she knew herself a bit better. She called her child back to her.

Pearl knew how to amuse herself and that's what she had been doing, making little boats out of birch-bark and giving them a cargo of snail and shells only to see them founder near the water's edge. She laid a jelly-fish out to melt in the warm sun and pelted beach-birds with stones, though she was a little upset when she saw she had hurt one. Just before her mother called her she got seaweed of various kinds and made herself a mermaid scarf and head-dress and as the final touch she added green eel-grass out of which she made a letter A.

That's when she heard her mother call her. She came dancing, laughing, and pointing her finger to the ornament upon her bosom.

"Pearl," said the mother, looking silently for a moment or two, "on you the green letter has no meaning. But do thou know what the letter means that I wear?"

"Yes, mother. It's the great letter **A**. You taught me that." She had that ugly knowing look on her face.

"Do you know, child, why your mother wears this letter?"

"Yes I do!" she said, looking brightly into her mother's face. "It's for the same reason that the minister keeps his hand over his heart!"

"And why is that?" asked Hester. "What has the letter to do with any heart except mine?"

"Now, mother, I have told you all I know," said Pearl, more seriously than she usually spoke. "Ask that old man you've been talking with, maybe he can tell you. Now, tell me what the scarlet letter means and why you wear it on your dress? And why does the minister keep his hand over his heart?"

She took her mother's hand in both her own and looked into her eyes with an earnestness rarely seen in this wild child. The thought occurred to Hester that she might really be looking for a deeper relationship and at this moment, as intelligently and as confidently as a child could, she was trying to establish mutual trust.

If so, this was Pearl in a different light. Up to this point, while Hester loved the child with the intensity of a sole affection, she had come to expect nothing from her but ceaseless change. She was an April breeze, kissing your cheek, chilling your heart, staying a while and then off on idle business elsewhere, promising prolonged gentleness and then producing gusts of passion and petulance.

But here she was, holding her mother's hand in her own and pouring out what looked and sounded like a plea for a deeper relationship. The thought gripped Hester that Pearl, with her remarkable precocity and acuteness, might already have come to the age when she could be made a friend and entrusted with as much of her mother's history as would be appropriate between a mother and her young daughter. There was no doubt that whatever chaos swirled in the child's character she had showed—from the very first— unflinching courage, an indomitable will and a sturdy pride that could be disciplined into self-respect. And she had a bitter scorn of humbug and what looked like insincerity. She possessed affections, too, though they needed time to ripen and gain sweetness. With all these in her favor, Hester thought, she must surely grow into a noble woman unless the evil she inherited from her mother was of absolutely mammoth proportions.

There was no doubt that Pearl had a marked preoccupation with the enigmatic scarlet letter and it seemed to be built into her.

As a tiny infant she couldn't keep her hands off it. Hester had often imagined that Providence was punishing her by giving the child this marked consciousness of the symbol but never until this moment had she thought it might also be a gift of mercy. If Pearl were brought to faith and trust and treated as such, perhaps she would be a spiritual messenger as well as an earthly child. Could it not be— Hester mused—could it not be that she had been sent to help her mother to overcome the once wild passion that still wasn't dead or asleep, but only imprisoned in her heart? These thoughts appealed to her so strongly that she felt as if they'd actually been whispered into her ear. And there was the child all this while, holding her mother's hand in her own, looking up at her and repeating the searching questions. "What does the letter mean, mother? Why do you wear it? And why does the minister keep his hand over his heart?" Hester snapped out of her reflecting and told herself that if laying all that on Pearl was the price for the child's sympathy and intimacy that she wasn't willing to pay it.

"Silly Pearl," she said, "what kind of questions are these? There are many things in this world that a child mustn't ask about. Anyway, what do I know of the minister's heart? And as for the scarlet letter, I wear it because it looks lovely, with its gold thread and beautiful colors." This was the first time she had lied about the symbol on her dress.

Among all the other things it might have been, it may have acted as a stern but guardian spirit, keeping her honest while keeping her on the straight and narrow; now she had weakened its power by denying its meaning. Had a new evil just crept into her or had an old one that had never been expelled just gained a new lease of life? As for Pearl, the earnestness soon passed out of her face.

But the aggravating child didn't see fit to let the matter drop. Two or three times as they headed home and again at suppertime she put the question. While Hester was putting her to bed she brought the matter up and once after she seemed to have fallen asleep, she looked up, with roguishness gleaming in her black eyes, and asked, "Mother, what does the scarlet letter mean?" And the next morning, as soon as her eyes were opened the nagging began again. "Mother? Mother! Why does the minister keep his hand over his heart?" Hester, infuriated by the constant badgering, turned on

162

her. "Hold your tongue, you undisciplined child! Stop harassing me or I'll lock you in that dark closet!"

16

A Forest Walk

She'd made up her mind that whatever it cost she was going to reveal to Mr. Dimmesdale the true identity and character of the man who had wormed his way into his life. She wasn't sure how it would work out for him but she couldn't imagine that things would be worse for him than now. How could that be? It was more difficult to get with him than she had anticipated because, for one thing, he kept himself to himself and though she searched in several places where she knew he walked he wasn't there when she got to them. Of course she could have gone to his study and that wouldn't have seemed strange because many troubled people made their way there. But that was just the problem, she didn't want to talk with him where they would likely be disturbed since she wasn't sure how he would be affected by the news. But more importantly, she wanted to be sure that Chillingworth wouldn't be around when she was speaking to him because both she and the minister would need the whole wide world to breathe in while this matter was thrashed out. Being alone with him in some out of the way place had its risks since if anyone saw them tongues would begin to wag but it seemed the lesser of two evils. Then she heard that the young minister had gone to visit the Apostle Eliot, among his Indian converts, and that he would probably return by a certain hour in the afternoon the next day.

The road they took became little more than a footpath that straggled on its way into the mystery of the dense forest. It was so dense that only now and then could you get a glimpse of the sky and Hester, with her tendency to be morbid, felt it hemming her in and stifling her like the moral wilderness she had been wandering in for so long. The chilly and somber day didn't help. The clouds were heavy and gray, broken here and there, allowing in occasional and brief bursts of brilliant sunlight that did little to generate warmth.

Her usual impudent and thoughtless self and still goading Hester about the scarlet symbol, Pearl said, "Mother, the sunshine doesn't seem to like you. When you come near it, it runs and hides. I think it's afraid of the letter on your bosom. There it is, watch! You stand here and I'll run and catch it. It won't run from me—for I wear nothing on my bosom yet!"

"I hope you never will child."

"And why not, mother?" asked Pearl, stopping short, just at the beginning of her race. "Will it not just come by itself when I'm grown woman?"

Weary of the subject and a little peeved, Hester said, "Run away, child, go catch the sunshine. It will soon be gone." Off she raced at a gallop and the doting mother couldn't help smiling when she did actually catch the sunshine and stood laughing in it, all bright and sparkling as she pranced and danced.

As her mother came close enough to step into the magic circle Pearl said, "It will go now." And sure enough, just as Hester stretched out her hand to grab some of it, it vanished. Pearl cackled, brimful of vigorous life and spirit and hadn't caught the disease of sadness that so many of the children in these days seem to inherit from their parents as surely as they inherit tuberculosis. Her unbridled energy was certainly a questionable charm because along with it there was a brittle and metallic luster to the child's character. She knew nothing of sympathy or tenderness and what she would need before she was mature was—what so many people need—a grief that should deeply touch her and make her more human. But she was very young and there was plenty of time yet for her but she was tiresome.

"Come on, Pearl, let's get off the path and sit down for a while and rest."

"I'm not tired, mother," she said. "But you sit down and you can tell me a story while you're resting."

"A story about what?"

"Oh, a story about the Dark One." Without a breath she poured out the words in a torrent. "Tell me how he haunts this forest, and carries a book with him, a big heavy book with iron clasps, and tell me how this ugly Dark One offers his book and iron pen to everybody that meets him here among the trees and how they are to write their names with their own blood and then how he puts his mark on their bosoms. Did you ever meet the Dark One, mother?" The torrent ended and there was a pause.

"And who told you this story, Pearl?" asked her mother.

"It was the old dame in the chimney corner, at the house where you watched last night," said the child. "But she thought I was asleep while she was talking about it. She said that a thousand and a thousand people have met him here and have written in his book and have his mark on them. And that that ugly tempered lady, old Mistress Hibbins, was one of them. And, mother, the old dame said that this scarlet letter was the Dark One's mark on you and that it glows like a red flame when you meet him at midnight here in the dark wood. Is it true, mother? And do you go to meet him in the nighttime?"

"Did you ever awake and find I wasn't there?" asked Hester.

"Not that I remember," said the child. "If you're afraid to leave me alone in our cottage you could take me along with you. I'd love to go! But, mother, tell me now! Is there such a Dark One? And did you ever meet him? And is this his mark?"

"Will you give me peace, if I tell you?" asked her mother.

"Yes, if you tell me everything."

"Once in my life I met the Dark One!" her mother said. "And this scarlet letter is his mark!"

As they talked they were walking further into the forest so that they wouldn't be seen from the road. They sat down on a gigantic pine tree that years earlier must have touched the sky. Now it lay covered with luxuriant moss in a little leaf-strewn dell with a stream running through it, the perfect resting-place for weary travelers.

They followed the stream with their eyes until it vanished in the depths and noted little pools and glistening stretches where the sun glanced in. It was all so mysterious and secretive and the voice of the stream only added a sad sort of babbling to the forest's unwillingness to be open and inviting. It was too much for Pearl.

"Oh, brook! You tiresome little brook!" she shouted, "Why are you so sad? Pluck up spirit and don't be all the time sighing and murmuring!" But the brook seemed to have nothing else to say. Swinging around she said, "What is this sad little brook saying, mother?"

"If you knew what it was to have a sorrow you would understand what the brook is saying," answered her mother. And then she hushed her, "I hear someone coming up the path. Look, I need you to play and leave me to speak this man."

"Is it the Dark Man?" the girl asked.

"Will you go and play, child?" repeated her mother, "But don't go far into the wood. And see to it that you come the first time I call you."

"Yes, mother, but if it's the Dark One, will you not let me stay for a moment and look at him, with his big book under his arm?"

"Go, silly child!" said her tormented mother. "It's not the Dark Man! You can't see him now through the trees but it's the minister!"

"And so it is!" she said, catching sight of him. "And, mother, look, he has his hand over his heart! Is it because, when the minister wrote his name in the book, the Dark Man set his mark there? But why does he not wear it outside, as you do?"

169

"Go now, child! And bother me another time," cried Hester Prynne, giving her a gentle push. "But, remember, stay where you can hear the noise of the stream."

Away she went and Hester Prynne stepped towards the footpath and saw the minister approach, he was entirely alone and leaning on a staff. He looked haggard and feeble and despondent, more noticeably so than ever and the gloomy setting only seemed to make him look worse. In town he couldn't keep from looking poorly but he always put on a brave face and acted better than he felt; but now that he was out of sight he didn't have the energy or feel the need to put on a front. He was a broken man who showed no sign that he had anything worth living for, and he kept his hand over his heart.

17

A Pastor and His Parish

He'd almost gone by before she could get up the courage to call him. "Arthur Dimmesdale!" she said, faintly at first, then louder, but hoarsely. "Arthur Dimmesdale!"

"Who's that?" he wanted to know. He stood more erect, not wanting anyone to see him in that stooped and tottering posture of a moment earlier. He peered through the trees and saw the somberly dressed figure. He stepped closer and caught sight of the scarlet letter. "Hester! Hester Prynne!' he said, "is it you? Is it really you? You're still alive?"

"Yes," she answered. "If what I have had this past seven years can be called life. And you, Arthur Dimmesdale, what about you, are you still alive?"

The strange mutual greeting; how do you explain it but as the result of the gloomy meeting-place, the gloomy hearts, the long absence from one another and the awkwardness of the moment? They struck each other as strange and unreal, a ghost of past days, a reminder of moments they wished had never been but could never be erased. The meeting conjured up a time they wished was still theirs but they knew that there was no going back. Fearful and trembling, he felt compelled to reach out and touch her with a hand that was as cold as death and found that hers was no warmer than his own. Cold as it was, the touch took away what was dreariest in the meeting— the sense of unreality and the feeling of utter loneliness. At least they now knew that when they woke in the mornings the other was still in the world and somehow that glad realization made a difference.

Without speaking another word and without thinking, they made their way into the woods and sat down in the little dell. Finally they spoke; it was small talk to ease away the awkwardness and open the door to other things. Step by step they moved into matters that lay deepest on their hearts.

"Hester," he said, "have you found peace?"

She smiled drearily, looking down upon her bosom. "Have you?"

"None—nothing but despair!" he muttered. "What else could I look for being what I am and leading a life like mine? If I were an atheist— a man without conscience, a wretch with coarse and brutal instincts— I might have found peace long before now. No, if I had been all that I never would have lost peace. But as matters stand with my soul, whatever good was in me, all the richest and best of

God's gifts, have only become sources of spiritual torment, Hester. I'm terribly miserable!"

"The people worship you. Surely you know that you do so much good among them! Does this bring you no comfort?"

"No, my dear, no, only more misery. Only more misery!" said the pathetic clergyman with a bitter smile. "The good that I appear to do? I have no faith in it. It can only be a delusion. What can a ruined soul like mine contribute to the redemption of other souls? What can a polluted soul do to help them be pure? Yes, the people's reverence," he said, as if to himself, "I wish it were scorn and hatred. Can you think it would console me, Hester, when I stand in my pulpit and see so many eyes turned upward to my face as if the light of heaven were beaming from it? I'm compelled to look out there and see them hungry for the truth and at the same time I'm compelled to look inward and face the lying reality of the one they idolize? I've laughed in bitter agony of heart at the difference between what I seem to be and what I really am! And Satan laughs too!"

"You wrong yourself in this," she said gently. "Your repentance has been deep and sore. You left your sin behind you a long time ago. Your present life is holy; every bit as holy as it seems in people's eyes. Are you saying there is no reality in the repentance sealed and witnessed by good works? You know better so why shouldn't it bring you peace?"

"No, Hester, no!" he persisted. "There's no substance in it. It's cold and dead and can do nothing for me! Of penance, now, of that I have enough! But of penitence there has been none! If there had been I would long ago have thrown off these preaching clothes and the mock holiness that goes with them and I'd have shown myself to mankind as they'll see me at the judgment-seat. You're fortunate, Hester, because you wear the scarlet letter openly on your breast! Mine burns in secret! You can't possibly know what a relief it is, after the torment of seven years of lying and cheating to look straight into the eye at someone who recognizes me for what I am! If I had one friend—or even my worst enemy!—anyone! to whom I could go when I'm deeply sickened by the praises of everyone around me, just to confess and be known as the vilest of all sinners—if I had that, I think my soul might keep itself alive. Even that much honesty would save me! But it's all falsehood, all emptiness, all death!"

Hester's heart beat faster; here was the perfect opportunity to tell him what she had vowed she would tell him. His very words begged her to open her mouth and still she hesitated to speak. He couldn't have expressed his pain and need more vehemently; and hadn't he just said that his soul could survive if he knew that there was someone who knew him for what he was? Her fear wasn't hard to understand but she mustn't let it silence her, so she spoke.

"You have a friend, the kind of friend you wished for just a moment ago. I'm that friend; you can weep over your sin with me. I'm your partner in it and we can weep together." Again she hesitated, but she dragged the words out with a supreme effort. "And you have had such an enemy for a long time; you live with him under the same roof!" There was a pause while the words registered with him and then the minister staggered to his feet, gasping for breath and clutching at his heart as if he would have torn it out of his chest.

174

"Aaah!" he groaned aloud before he shouted, "What are you saying? An enemy! And under my own roof! What do you mean?" It was too late now; she couldn't take the words back. But what she always thought she understood she now realized she hadn't truly known. Not really, not with a full awareness. It was only now that she saw his horror and heard his panic that she saw the hurt and loss she had subjected him to in those seven years. Seven years? Seven years? How could she have let him lie under it for seven minutes? Seven years under Chillingworth's malignancy and cruelty? She gave him seven years to practice and perfect his ways to abuse and wound this young man. For seven years she had given him permission to try this torment and that, to measure the agony and if he thought it wasn't enough he had the freedom to try something else. Seven years she allowed the twisted old hypocrite to soothe and sweet talk, to pretend and deceive and...violate! And if he had been torturing someone with a stronger temperament, one not so sensitive as Arthur, the pain while real would not have been as awful. But she knew how the young man was and still she gave the crippled old abuser the key to Arthur's heart.

She thought she was helping him but since the night of his vigil she now read the situation more accurately. She knew then that he was no match for what the skillful man had in mind. His continual presence, the secret poison of his malice that infected all the air around him, his authorized interference with the minister's physical and spiritual infirmities—by these he kept Arthur's conscience in fever and turmoil. He had no intention of curing him by keeping the conscience alive! He meant to disorganize and corrupt him and when he had grown tired of the game and bored with the victim, he

175

would drive him to insanity and after that to eternal alienation from the Good and True. She shuddered.

This was the ruin to which she had brought the man she once— the man she still loved so passionately! She wished she could fall down dead at his feet. It was time to beg while explaining and explain while begging.

"Oh, Arthur forgive me! I've always been truthful—always—but when it came to your welfare, your good name and your good work I couldn't bring myself to speak. It was for you I went along with deception. Yes, yes, I knew a lie is never good even if speaking the truth might result in death!" Her head was reeling now. "Do you understand what I'm trying to say? That old man—the doctor—the man who calls himself Roger Chillingworth—he...he...was my husband!"

There, she'd said it! The minister looked at her with all that violence of passion that lived alongside and intertwined with the gentler and softer qualities in his complex nature. It was at this point that Satan had attacked him over seven years ago and won, and it was by this entrance he hoped to gain complete control of the whole person. Hester had never experienced a more savage or fiercer frown than the one she now faced. While it lasted it was a horrific transfiguration, but made feeble by suffering, he didn't have the energy to sustain it. He sank to the ground and buried his face in his hands and rocked backwards and forwards.

"I might have known it," he murmured. "I did know it! The secret was told to me in the natural recoil of my heart the first time I saw him and every time I have seen him since. Why did I not understand? Oh, Hester Prynne, you have no earthly idea of all the horror of this thing! And the shame, the indecency and the horrible ugliness of this exposure of a sick and guilty heart to the very one that would gloat over it and pry into it! Woman, woman, you are accountable for this! I can't forgive you!"

"You will forgive me!" she cried, flinging herself on the ground beside him. "Let God punish! You will forgive!"

With sudden and desperate tenderness she threw her arms around him and pressed his head against her chest. He tried to get free but she wouldn't let him go in case he should look at her again in that harsh, merciless way. The entire world had frowned on her— for seven long years it had frowned on her— and still she bore it all, never once turning away her firm, sad eyes. Heaven had frowned on her too and she hadn't died. But the frown of this pale, weak, sinful, and sorrow-stricken man was more than she could bear and go on living!

"Will you forgive me?" she repeated, over and over again. "Will you not frown at me? Will you please forgive me?"

Forever came and went and then out of an abyss of sadness from which all anger had been purged he said, "I do forgive you, Hester. I freely forgive you this very moment. May God forgive us both! I thought I was—I thought we were—the worst sinners in the world but we're not, Hester. There's one that's worse than even the polluted priest! That old man's revenge has been blacker than my sin. He has violated, in cold blood, the sanctity of a human heart. You and I, Hester, we never did that!"

"Never, never!" she whispered. "What we did had a consecration of its own. We felt it so! We said so to each other. Have you forgotten it?"

"Hush, Hester!" he said, rising from the ground. "No; I've not forgotten!" They sat down again, side by side, hand clasped in hand on the mossy trunk of the fallen tree. Life had never brought them a gloomier hour; it was the point that their pathway had so long been leading them to and it had been growing darker the farther they walked on it.

And yet the path had had a charm that made them linger there, and claim another moment and another and then another. The forest looked on at them and creaked with a wind that was passing through it. The branches moved heavily above their heads while one solemn old tree groaned dolefully to another, telling the sad story of the pair that sat beneath, and maybe whispering to one another about evil to come.

And still they lingered. How dreary the forest-track looked that led back to the settlement where she must take up again the burden of her isolation and the minister the hollow mockery of his communion—one feeling the hurt of being separated and the other wishing he were separated! So they lingered a little while longer. No golden dawn had ever been as precious as the present gloom of this dark forest. Here, seen only by his eyes the scarlet letter need not burn into the breast of the fallen woman! Here seen only by her eyes, Arthur Dimmesdale, false before God and man might be true for one moment! He was scared by a thought that suddenly occurred to him and brought misery rushing back like a torrent in a ravine.

"Hester! Roger Chillingworth knows you plan to reveal his true character. Will he decide then to reveal our secret? What course will his revenge take now?"

"There's an unwillingness in his nature to be open about things," she said thoughtfully; "and it has grown on him in these last seven years. I don't think it likely that he will betray the secret. Besides, he has much to lose. No doubt he will seek other means to satisfy his evil passion."

"How will I be able to survive breathing the same air with him?" Arthur groaned, shrinking within himself, and pressing his hand nervously against his heart. "Think for me, Hester! You're strong. Tell me what to do!"

"You mustn't live with him any longer," she said slowly and firmly. Your heart mustn't be under his evil eye any longer!"

"That would be far worse than death! But how am I to avoid it? What choice do I have? Should I lie down and die here?"

Hester began to sob. "Will you die just because you're weak? There is no reason for you to think this way!"

"The judgment of God is on me," said the conscience-stricken priest. "It is too powerful for me to struggle with!"

"Heaven would show mercy," she insisted, "if you only had the strength to take advantage of it."

"You be strong for me! Advise me what to do." He groaned again.

She fixed her eyes on him, a man whose spirit was so shattered and subdued that it could hardly hold itself erect.

"Is the world so tiny that it's restricted to that town? Not long ago it was wild spot in the wilderness and has it now become the whole world? This forest track might lead back to the town but it leads elsewhere! A few miles from here there are places where no white man has ever walked. You would be free there! A few miles journey

179

would bring you from a world where you have been unbelievably wretched to one where you can be happy again! Are there not enough places in all this boundless world to hide your heart from the eyes of Roger Chillingworth?"

"Yes, Hester; but only under the fallen leaves!" replied the minister, with the sad smile of a man too tired to want to try.

"But we don't have to stay here!" she said with some impatience. We could go back to the old country and live in some remote rural village or lose ourselves in London—or in Germany, France or in Italy—somewhere, where he couldn't find us! And anyway, what have you in common with all these iron men and their opinions? They have kept the better part of you in bondage too long already!"

"None of that can ever be!" answered the minister, listening as if he were being asked to believe a dream. "I am powerless to go. Wretched and sinful as I am I believe this is where God wants me to be, where he has placed me. Lost as my own soul is, I must continue to do what I can for other human souls! I don't dare desert my post though I've been an unfaithful sentry whose sure reward is death and dishonor."

"You're crushed under this seven year weight of misery," she said, determined to buoy him up with her own energy. "But you'll leave it all behind you if you take the forest-path away from here. You won't take it with you as cargo if you decide to cross the sea. Leave this wreck and ruin here where it has happened. Meddle no more with it! Start fresh! There's happiness to be enjoyed! There's good to be done! Exchange this false life of yours for a true one. Be a missionary and teacher and apostle of the Red men. Or be a scholar and a sage among the wisest and the most renowned of the cultivated world.

"Preach! Write! Act! Do anything, except lie down and die! Give up the name Arthur Dimmesdale, make yourself another, a high one that you can wear without fear or shame. Why should you delay one more day in the torment that has gnawed into your life and has taken the will and power from you? Stay here and it will leave you powerless even to repent! Get up and leave. Now!"

His eyes lit up, set alight by her enthusiasm but within seconds he flagged again, she had wasted her breath.

"Oh, Hester, you tell a man to run a race whose knees are tottering beneath him! I must die here! There is not the strength or courage left in me to face another world alone!" It was the last expression of the despondency of an utterly broken man. He repeated the word—"Alone, Hester!"

"But you won't go alone!" she whispered. With that, not another word was spoken.

18

A Flood of Sunshine

Arthur Dimmesdale looked long at Hester with hope and joy reflected on his face but he was too weak not to feel fear as well. She frightened him with her boldness when she spoke plainly of things he only hinted at but didn't dare to voice. Hinted at? He hardly dared to let himself think such things.

But she had courage and wasn't shackled as he was by his environment and training. For years she had been outlawed from society and that left her free to think without its interference or threats, free to think in a way that he was incapable of. She had wandered without rule or guidance in a moral wilderness as vast and as shadowy as the untamed forest that surrounded them. Her intellect and heart hadn't been domesticated so she roamed as freely as the wild Indian in his woods and for years she had looked from this point of view at human institutions. Within she criticized whatever priests or legislators had established with as much irreverence as the Indian would feel, whether it was the judicial robe, the pillory, the gallows, the fireside or the church. Her fate had set her free in so many ways.

The scarlet letter was her passport into regions where other women dared not go. Shame, despair, solitude; these had been her teachers—stern and wild ones—and they had made her strong. But not everything they taught her was true! The minister, on the other hand, had never experienced anything that was calculated to lead him beyond the perimeter of generally received laws. Yes, in a single instance he had so fearfully transgressed one of the most sacred of them. But this had been a sin of passion, not of principle, nor even purpose. He loved the law he had broken and had not set himself in conscious defiance to it nor did he seek to justify his having broken it. The reverse was true. Since that wretched time he had watched with morbid zeal not only his actions—for it was easy to arrange those—but also each breath of emotion and his every thought. As a man who had greatly sinned he kept his conscience alive and painfully sensitive by ceaselessly picking off the scab and refusing to allow the wound to heal. The clergymen of that day stood at the head of the social system and this meant he was only the more bound by its regulations, its principles and even its prejudices. As a priest, the framework of his order inevitably hemmed him in. His position made it difficult, if not nearly impossible to think daring things but it was his sin that sealed his fate.

To think differently, to think boldly—not to say "bravely"—would now look as if he were in some way justifying his sin or minimizing the punishment due. The very thought that some would think this of him was unbearable! So here he was strapped by a rigid religion and a nature too high strung to a conscience that had run amok and had taken over the reigns of his life. It no longer served the healthy, even essential, function for which it existed and instead of sounding a warning it endlessly screeched condemnation. Blinded by his training and place in society and church he wasn't able to see that it was malfunctioning.

On the contrary, and this added profoundly to his misery, he saw it as the voice of God. With such a conscience he might have supposed he was safer than if he hadn't sinned at all. But if it kept him virtuous by a careful avoidance of evil it destroyed his life, his peace and that ensured that he would never be free to think.

So it appears that the whole seven years as renegade and object of shame had prepared Hester Prynne for this very hour, enabling her to think and plan daringly. But Arthur Dimmesdale! If he were to fall again what plea could be urged in extenuation of his crime? None! ["See? This was his nature and purpose all along! That we didn't see it only shows how well he hid his tracks and how skilled he is in hypocrisy."] What difference would it make if someone said he had been broken down and made feeble by long and excruciating mental suffering, that his mind was darkened and confused by the very remorse that daily sliced through it like a ploughshare? Who would care that conscience might find it hard to strike the balance between fleeing as a known criminal and remaining as a hypocrite? Would it matter to anyone in such a

185

church and society that it was human to want to escape not only death but also infamy? Would there be one—a single, solitary person—that would stand up and remind his critics that finally, after long years of purgatory at the hands of an enemy, there appeared to this poor pilgrim on his dreary and desert path, faint, sick and miserable—that there appeared to him a glimpse of human affection and sympathy that offered a new life and a true one in exchange for the existence he endured? But this stern and sad truth must be spoken: once sin has made the breach into the human soul it can't be repaired in this life. The soul may be watched and guarded so that the enemy can't force his way into the citadel but he did breach it once. He may have to choose some other avenue to gain entrance again but there is still the ruined wall and near it, eyeing it and musing over the possibilities there's the stealthy tread of the foe that looks to repeat the triumph he hasn't forgotten.

Well, the struggle, if there was one, need not be described. It's enough to say that the clergyman resolved to flee and not alone.

"If in all these past seven years," he thought, "I could recall one instant of peace or hope I would yet endure in light of that single gift and proof of Heaven's mercy. But now—since I'm irrevocably doomed—why shouldn't I snatch the comfort allowed to the condemned criminal before his execution? Or, if this is the path to a better life, as Hester thinks, I can't do worse by pursuing it!" He admitted this to himself also, "I can't live any longer without her companionship. She is so powerful to sustain me and so tender to soothe me!" The very thought of this stabbed at his heart. "O you, to whom I dare not lift my eyes, is there any hope at all that you will pardon me?"

"You will go!" said Hester calmly, as his eyes and thoughts returned to her.

The decision once made had an exhilarating effect on a prisoner just escaped from the dungeon of his own heart. He was breathing the wild, free atmosphere of an unredeemed, unchristian and lawless region and it drove his spirit to the sky. Because he couldn't be other than deeply religious, the sense of joy and peace made him feel nearer to God and heaven than all the years of misery when he groveled on the earth.

"Is this joy I feel again?" he said in amazement. "I thought the very possibility of it was dead in me! Oh, Hester, you're my better angel! I flung myself sick, sin-stained and sorrow-blackened down on these forest leaves and I feel I've risen up all made new, with new powers and a renewed hunger to glorify him that has been merciful! This is already the better life! Why did we not find it sooner?"

"Let's not look back," she said. "The past is gone! Why should we dwell on it? See! With this symbol I undo it all and make it as if it had never been!" As she said it she undid the clasp of the scarlet letter and threw it as far as she could among the withered leaves. It fell just short of the stream, glittering like a lost jewel waiting to be found by some wanderer.

The stigma was gone! She heaved a long, deep sigh and maybe as the breath left her so did all the suppressed shame and anguish. O exquisite relief! She hadn't known the weight until she felt the freedom! And since she was saying goodbye to the past she took off the formal cap that confined her hair and down it fell on to her shoulders, dark and rich and abundant, giving the charm of softness to her features. Back around her mouth and out of her eyes was a radiant and tender smile that seemed to be gushing from the very heart of womanhood. A crimson flush was glowing on her cheek that had been long so pale. Her sensuous youth and the whole richness of her beauty came back from what men call the irrevocable past.

Hope and beauty and happiness all combined in an experience she had never known—all these in the magic circle of this hour. And as if the gloom of the earth and sky had been only the reflection of these two mortal hearts it vanished when their sorrow vanished. All at once the sun poured a flood of glory down on the dismal forest, gladdening each green leaf and transforming the yellow fallen ones to gleaming gold. The little brook that a while ago wound its way into the heart of gloomy mystery now looked cheerful and led to joyful mystery.

This—so it seemed—was how Nature felt. Wild, heathen Nature that was never subjugated by human law or illuminated by higher truth gave its approval on the bliss of these two spirits! Love, newborn or roused from a death-like sleep will always create sunshine, filling the heart so full of radiance that it overflows on the outward world. If the forest had remained gloomy in the eyes of the two lovers it would still have been brighter.

"You must know Pearl!" she gasped, remembering. "Our little Pearl! You've seen her but you'll see her differently now. She's a strange child! I hardly understand her but you'll love her dearly as I do and you will advise me how to deal with her!"

"Do you think the child will be glad to know me?" he asked. "I've long shrunk back from children. They're not at ease with me. I've even been afraid of Pearl!"

"Ah, that was sad. But she will love you dearly and you her. She can't be far away." She called her.

"There she is, standing in the sunshine on the other side of the stream, see? So you think she will love me?" Hester smiled, and called her again and she heard. She hadn't found it difficult to pass the hours. With her mother's call she came.

Slowly—for she saw the clergyman and more!

19

The Child at the Brookside

"**Y**ou'll love her dearly," she repeated as she and the minister sat watching Pearl. "Isn't she beautiful? And do you see how she is able to make those simple flowers look like jewels on her? She's a very gifted child, but I know where she got that from!"

"Do you know, Hester," he replied, incapable of leaving his sad story behind for very long, "that child has caused me many an anxious feeling? I thought—and how pathetic of me to think such a thing—I thought she looked so much like me that people would know whose child she was just my looking. But now with the fear gone it's obvious that she is so much more like you."

"A little longer," she said, "and you won't have to be afraid how much like you she is."

Slowly approaching them was the visible tie that united them. Whatever the clues revealed in the child, the reputation of this good man—good in so many wonderful ways—had made it impossible for any one to even think there was a connection.

However sinful their behavior had been, when they looked at this person coming toward them they had no doubt that their earthly lives and future destinies were joined. Being aware of this they looked at the child not simply as a father and a mother would—the truth about her invested her with a meaning greater than herself and in that respect she was somehow a revelation. Pleased and yet appalled they looked at her with something like awe.

"Relax and act as normal as possible," Hester whispered. "Don't let her sense you awkward or too eager to embrace her. Our Pearl is a skittish and fantastic little elf sometimes. She finds it hard to appreciate emotion, especially when she doesn't fully understand the why and wherefore. But the child has strong affections! She loves me and will love you!"

"I dread and long for this at the same time," he said, stealing a glance at Hester. "Now remember what I told you, children don't quickly take to me. They won't climb on my knee or prattle in my ear. Even little babies—" he left the sentence unfinished. Then, to assure himself, "Yet Pearl has been kind to me! The first time—you know it well, at the scaffold! And then at the house of old Governor Bellingham."

"I remember," she whispered, "and you pleaded so bravely in her behalf and mine! I remember it and so will Pearl. Don't be afraid, she may be strange and shy at first but she'll soon learn to love you!"

By this time Pearl had reached the farther side of the stream and stood gazing silently at Hester and the clergyman who still sat together on the mossy tree-trunk waiting for her. Where she stopped the stream happened to form a pool so smooth and quiet that it reflected a perfect image of her. The sun shone on her and in the pool stood another child—another and yet the same—surrounded with the golden light. If asked she couldn't have explained it but Hester felt cut off from Pearl, as if the child had entered another mode of life, a realm that separated her from her mother. And for that reason the child, glorious though she looked, anxiously wanted to return but wasn't able. Both mother and daughter sensed the gulf! But the gulf wasn't quite of Pearl's making. When she had rambled from her mother's side they were two—now there were three. A third admitted within the circle of the mother's feelings changed the situation of all three and the bizarre child was uncertain of her place because somehow it had affected her understanding of who she was.

"You would think that that stream is the boundary between two worlds," Arthur said. "Please hurry her, my nerves are beginning to give way."

"Come on, Pearl!" said Hester encouragingly, and stretching out both her arms. "You are such a slow coach! When have you ever been so slow? Here's a friend of mine who wants to be your friend too. You'll have twice as much love from now on as I can give you by myself! Come on, jump! You can leap like a young deer! Jump the stream."

She didn't respond in any way to these honey-sweet expressions and remained on the other side of the brook. She fixed her bright wild eyes on her mother one moment and on the preacher the next and then looked at them as one. How did they relate to each other? In his extreme nervousness Arthur's hand had crept over his heart as he felt the child's eyes burning into him. Then suddenly she stretched out her hand, index finger extended in a show of authority and evidently pointing towards her mother's breast. And beneath her, in the mirror of the stream, a second flower-girdled figure joined in the finger pointing.

"You odd child! Why won't you come to me?" shouted Hester.

Pearl still pointed with her forefinger and a frown like a stern old woman gathered on her brow—a frown all the more shocking because it was not the frown of a child. As her mother still kept gesturing to her smiling—or at least trying to smile—the child became increasingly angry, pointing wildly and stamping her foot, making it clear she would not be appeased.

"You come here young lady or I'll be angry with you!" cried her mother. She was used to such behavior but this was the wrong moment and she was especially anxious for her to behave properly.

"You come here or I will come and get you." But Pearl wasn't moved by her mother's threats any more than she was softened by her appeals. She suddenly burst into a fit of passion, gesturing violently and shrieking at the top of her lungs. The forest reverberated on all sides! In the midst of all she continued to point that forefinger at Hester's bosom.

"I see what's wrong with the child," Hester whispered dejectedly to the clergyman, "I no longer look like her mother. She has never

194

seen me look like this." Arthur, by now a bundle of nerves, begged her to pacify the child if there was any way she could do it.

The raging girl had won. "Pearl," the beaten Hester said, "look down near your feet! There, on this side of the brook!" The child looked and there lay the scarlet letter.

"Bring it to me!" said Hester.

"You come and get it!" answered Pearl.

"Was there ever such a child?" Hester said to the minister as she rose. "Oh, I have much to tell you about her! Anyway, she's right as regards this hateful token. I need to wear it a little longer—only a few days longer—until we've left this region and look back on it as a land we dreamed about. The forest can't hide this thing! The ocean will take it from my hand and swallow it up for ever!"

She went, picked it up and fastened it again to her dress. She did it hopefully, but though she had said a moment ago that she would drown it in the deep sea there was a sense of inevitable doom on her as she put it back on. She had flung it from her, had drawn an hour's free breath and here again was the scarlet misery glittering on the old spot! Now she had to gather up the heavy tresses of her hair and cram them back beneath her cap. With the return of the symbol a withering spell was undoing her beauty and the warmth and richness of her womanhood departed like fading sunshine and a gray shadow seemed to take its place.

When the dreary change was made she extended her hand to Pearl. "Do you know your mother now, child?" she asked with some resentment but with a subdued tone. "Will you come now and recognize your mother, now that she has shame written on her, now that she is sad?"

The child's voice rang out, "Yes, now I will!" and she came bounding across the stream and threw her arms around her mother. "Now you're my mother again! And I'm your Pearl!" In a move of unusual tenderness she drew down her mother's head and kissed her brow and both her cheeks. But then—by a kind of necessity that seemed to compel this child to take back what she might have give—Pearl reached up and kissed the scarlet letter too.

"How cruel of you!" said Hester. "When you have shown me a little love you mock and hurt me!"

The little girl ignored the remark. "Why is the minister sitting there?"

"He wants to say hello to you," replied her mother. "Come and ask his blessing. He loves you Pearl and he loves your mother also. Will you not love him? Come on, he's really longing to greet you!"

"Does he love us?" said Pearl, looking up with a skeptical look. "Will he go back into the town with us hand in hand, the three of us, together?"

"Not now. But before long he will walk hand in hand with us. We'll have a home and fireside of our own and you will sit on his knee and he will teach you many things and you'll love him, won't you?"

But all this talk of firesides and sitting on knees had little appeal to this child. "And will he always keep his hand over his heart?" she asked dryly.

"Silly child, what sort of question is that!" exclaimed her disappointed mother. "Come and ask his blessing!" But, whether it was jealousy, which seems to be an instinct in every petted child towards a dangerous rival, or whatever it was, Pearl wouldn't go

196

near him. Her mother had virtually to drag her to the man and he—painfully embarrassed—hoping that a kiss might prove helpful leaned over and kissed her forehead. Pearl immediately broke away from her mother and running to the brook she bent over it, furiously bathing her forehead until the unwelcome kiss was washed off. From then on she stayed on her own, silently watching Hester and the clergyman while they talked and worked out their plans for the immediate future.

They left the dell in its solitude among the dark old trees. And the melancholy brook still softly babbled its sad stories. It was no more cheerful now that they were gone than it had been before they came.

20

The Minister in a Maze

As Arthur left he glanced back, half expecting to see only an outline of the mother and the child, slowly dissolving into the twilight of the woods. He found it hard to believe that so great a change of fortune in his life was real. But there was Hester in her gray dress still standing beside the tree-trunk and there was Pearl capering around on the bank of the stream, normal again now that the intruder was gone. So the minister hadn't fallen asleep and dreamed it all! He went back over and more thoroughly defined the plans that Hester and he had sketched for their departure. They had determined that the Old World with its crowds and cities offered them a more certain and available refuge than the wilds of New England or all America—a white couple with a child living among the Indians would attract attention. In the few settlements of Europeans scattered thinly along the seaboard they were more likely to come across inquisitive people and some that had heard the story of a vanishing minister, a child and a notorious woman. Then there was the clergyman's health to think of. He wasn't adequate for the hardships of a forest life. No, his gifts, culture and his entire development would secure him a home only in the heart of civilization and refinement. For all these reasons this was the best choice and it so happened that a ship lay in the harbor. It was one of those numerous but not highly reputable cruisers that roamed over the sea and asked no questions about cargo or reasons for travel. This vessel had recently arrived from the Spanish Main and within three days time would sail for Bristol.

Hester—as a self-enlisted Sister of Charity had made the acquaintance of the captain and crew—could secure passage for two individuals and a child and no one beyond the captain and crew would be any the wiser.

The minister had anxiously inquired from Hester the precise time of the vessel's departure. On the fourth day from the present the ship would be steaming its way toward Bristol. "The timing couldn't be better!" he told himself. The day before it was due to sail he was to preach the Election Sermon. This was a grand occasion and the clergyman chosen to make the address was greatly honored. He couldn't have chosen a better occasion and time to terminate his professional career if he had arranged it himself. "At least, they'll say of me," thought this exemplary man, "that I leave no public duty undone or poorly done!" Sadly, he was deceiving himself. A subtle disease had long been eating into the real substance of his character.

No man can wear one face to himself and another to the public for any considerable period without finally wondering which one was the true one.

It's no surprise that when he left after his meeting with Hester he had new physical energy that meant his journey to town was swift.

The woods seemed wilder and less trodden than he remembered them on his outward journey but he leaped across waterlogged places, pushed himself through the clinging underbrush, climbed the hills, plunged into the hollows and overcame all the difficulties of the track with an ease that astonished him. He couldn't help thinking how feeble he had been and how many times he had to pause for breath over the same ground only two days before. As he drew near the town it struck him how changed familiar objects were. It felt like he hadn't seen the town in years! True, he was able to recognize the outlines of the place with all the peculiarities of the houses, the gablepeaks, weathercocks and such. Just the same, things were not the same! And the acquaintances he met, they didn't look older or younger, the beards of the aged were no whiter and the creeping baby of yesterday wasn't walking on his feet today. It was impossible to describe in what way they differed from people he had seen just recently and yet the minister's deepest sense seemed to tell him they had changed! It was the same as he passed under the walls of his own church. The building was the same but altogether different and his mind churned between two ideas. Either he had seen it only in a dream before or he was merely dreaming now.

The truth is, nothing had changed externally but a profound and important change had taken place in Dimmesdale. A single momentous day had affected his consciousness as profoundly as if he had experienced a lapse of years. It was the same town as before but a different minister came out of the forest. He might have said to the friends who greeted him, "I'm not the man you take me for! I left him back there in the forest, lost in a secret dell by a mossy tree trunk near a melancholy stream! Go seek your minister there if you don't believe me, and see if his emaciated figure, his thin cheek, his white, heavy, pain-wrinkled brow isn't lying there like a cast-off garment!" No doubt his friends would have insisted, "No, no, you yourself are the man for we can see you with our own eyes!" But they would have been wrong and he would have been right! Before Mr. Dimmesdale reached home he had further proof that he was not the same man. To his horror he discovered that his inner kingdom was in the process of reconstruction. Nothing short of that could account for the impulses that now raced through this unfortunate and startled minister's mind. At every step he felt the drive to do some strange, wild, wicked thing or other. He sensed that at one and the same time he had no power to keep them out and yet that he was fully responsible for allowing them in. It was as if there were two selves inside him. One that opposed the wild and wicked impulses and another, more profound than his better self, and out of this one the impulses flowed.

For instance, he met one of his own deacons. The good old man addressed him with the paternal affection that his age, holy character and standing in the church warranted. In addition to this

his attitude toward the younger man was one of almost worshipping respect.

There never was a more beautiful example of how the majesty of age and wisdom might subject itself without loss of dignity and honor to someone it thought to be more gifted. During a conversation of some two or three minutes with this excellent and aged deacon, the Reverend Dimmesdale could barely keep himself from uttering certain blasphemous suggestions that rose into his mind respecting the communion-supper. He absolutely trembled and turned as pale as ashes in case his tongue would let them loose. And yet, even with this terror in his heart he could hardly keep from laughing to imagine how the sanctified patriarchal deacon would have been petrified by his minister's impiety.

Hurrying along the street the Reverend Mr. Dimmesdale encountered the oldest female member of his church, a most pious and exemplary old dame, poor, widowed, lonely, nearly deaf and with a heart full of memories about her husband, children and friends—all long dead. This devout old soul bore her sorrows with solemn joy by feeding herself continually on the truths of Scripture. And since Mr. Dimmesdale had taken her in charge, nothing was of more earthly or heavenly comfort than to be refreshed with a word of warm, fragrant, heaven-breathing Gospel truth from his beloved lips spoken into her dulled but rapturously attentive ear. But on this occasion, up to the moment when putting his lips to the old woman's ear the only thing he could think of saying was a brief and unanswerable argument against the immortality of the human soul. If he had shouted that into her ear this aged sister would probably have dropped down dead at his feet.

What he really did whisper the minister could never afterwards recollect. Whatever it was he said—or whatever she thought he said—when he looked back he saw an expression of divine gratitude and ecstasy that seemed like the shine of the celestial city on her wrinkled face.

Very soon after he met the youngest sister of them all. It was a maiden newly-won—and won by the Dimmesdale's own sermon on the Sabbath after his vigil. She was fair and pure as a lily that had bloomed in Paradise. The minister knew that she loved him madly and that she enshrined him within the stainless sanctity of her heart that hung its snowy curtains about his image. She gave religion the warmth of love and gave love a religious purity. Satan that afternoon had surely led the poor young girl away from her mother's side and thrown her into the pathway of this sorely tempted—or, this lost and desperate man. As she came near, the arch-fiend whispered to him to drop into her tender heart a germ of evil that would blossom and bear evil and ugly fruit. He had such a sense of power over this virgin soul, trusting him as she did, that he knew he could rot the entire field of innocence with one wicked look and gain the opposite of innocence with only a word. So with a mightier struggle than he had yet faced he held his Geneva cloak before his face and hurried past her without a sign of recognition. She ransacked her conscience— which, like her pocket or her workbag was full of harmless little matters—and took herself to task, poor thing, for a thousand imaginary faults. The next morning she went about her household duties with swollen eyes.

Before the minister had time to celebrate his victory over this last temptation he was conscious of another impulse, more ludicrous and almost as horrible. He longed to stop in the road and teach some very wicked words to a knot of little Puritan children who were playing there and that were just learning to talk. He denied himself this as unworthy of his status and then he met a drunken seaman, one of the ship's crew from the Spanish Main. Since he had so valiantly resisted all the other wickedness, poor Dimmesdale longed at least to shake hands with the tarry black-guard and tell a few dirty jokes and let loose a volley of good, round, solid, satisfactory and heaven-defying oaths! It wasn't a better principle that kept him from it but partly his natural good taste and his clerical habits that carried him safely through the last crisis.

"Why am I thinking this way? Am I mad? Or am I given over utterly to the Devil? Did I make a contract with him in the forest and sign it with my blood? Is that why these foul imaginings are filling my brain?" He thumped his forehead in distress.

At that very moment old Mistress Hibbins, the reputed witch-lady was passing by. She made a very grand appearance, with her high headdress, a rich gown of velvet, and a ruff done up with the famous yellow starch. Anne Turner, her special friend, had taught her the secret of the yellow starch before Anne had been hanged for Sir Thomas Overbury's murder. Whether or not the witch had read the minister's thoughts she came to a full stop, looked shrewdly into his face, smiled craftily and began a conversation (though she didn't have much time for clergymen).

"So, reverend sir, you made a visit into the forest," observed the witch-lady, nodding her high headdress at him. "Be sure to let me know the next time and I will be proud to keep you company. Without claiming too much importance for myself my good word would get you a fair reception from the potentate there, the one you know of."

"I profess, madam," answered the clergyman, with a grave bow, such as the lady's rank demanded and his own good breeding made imperative, "I profess, on my conscience and character that I have no idea what you are talking about. I didn't go into the forest to seek a potentate and neither do I at any future time intend to go there to gain the favor of such a person. My one and only object was to greet that pious friend of mine, the Apostle Eliot, and rejoice with him over the many precious souls he has won from heathendom!"

The old witch-lady cackled with laughter, still nodding her high headdress at the minister. "Well, of course, we must talk like that in the daytime! You carry it off like an old hand! But at midnight and in the forest we'll have other talk together!" She moved on with her aged stateliness but she kept looking back and smiling at him, like someone that knew what she knew but was content to leave it unsaid.

"Is that what I've done? Have I sold myself to the fiend they say this yellow-starched and velveted old hag has chosen for her prince and master?" the preacher muttered to himself.

The wretched minister! He had made a bargain very like it! Tempted by a dream of happiness he had yielded himself with deliberate choice to what he knew was deadly sin—that he had never done before. And the infection of that sin had rapidly spread through his moral system. It had stupefied all blessed impulses and galvanized into life a whole brotherhood of bad ones. Scorn, bitterness, unprovoked malignity, gratuitous desire of evil, ridicule of whatever was good and holy—all these awoke to tempt him even while they frightened him. And his encounter with old Mistress Hibbins, if the report is true, showed that she saw in him sympathy and fellowship with wicked mortals and the world of perverted spirits.

By this time he had reached his house and hurrying up the stairs he took refuge in his study. The minister was glad to have reached this shelter without first betraying himself to the world by any of those strange and wicked eccentricities to which he had been tempted. He entered the accustomed room, looked around him on its books, its windows, its fireplace and the tapestries on the walls with the same sense of strangeness he had experienced earlier. Here he had studied and written; here he had gone through fasts and vigils and come out half-alive. Here he had tried to pray and here he had borne a hundred thousand agonies! There was the Bible, in its rich old Hebrew, with Moses and the Prophets speaking to him and God's voice through all of them.

There on the table with the inky pen beside it was an unfinished sermon with a sentence broken in the middle when his thoughts had dried up. He knew that it was himself, the thin and white-cheeked minister who had done and suffered these things and written some of the Election Sermon! But he seemed to stand apart and eye this former self with scornful pity and half-envious curiosity. That self was gone. Another man had returned out of the forest—a wiser one—with knowledge of hidden mysteries that the simplicity of the earlier one never could have gained. A bitter kind of knowledge that! While he mused, a knock came at the door of the study and the minister said, "Come in!" He knew that he would see an evil spirit.

And so he did! It was old Roger Chillingworth that entered. The minister stood white and speechless with one hand on the Hebrew Scriptures and the other spread on his chest.

"Welcome home, reverend sir," said the physician "And how did you find that godly man, the Apostle Eliot?" Not waiting for an answer he said, "But I think, dear sir, you look pale, as if the travel through the wilderness had been too sore for you. Will you need me to help to put you in heart and strength to preach your Election Sermon?"

"No, I don't think so," rejoined the Reverend Mr. Dimmesdale. "My journey, and the sight of the holy Apostle there, and the free air that I have breathed have done me good after being so long confined in my study. I don't think I'll need any more of your drugs, my kind physician, good as they are and offered by your friendly hand."

All this time Roger Chillingworth was looking at the minister with the grave and intent regard of a physician towards his patient. But in spite of this outward show the minister suspected that the old man knew, or at least, confidently guessed, what had happened when he had met with Hester Prynne. The physician sensed that in the minister's regard he was no longer a trusted friend but his bitterest enemy. That being the case you might have thought that the whole matter would be laid out in the open, but no. It's strange how long it takes some people to do that; they circle and avoid and approach and then retire. The minister didn't really expect Chillingworth to speak of the matter in express words but the physician, in his dark way, crept frightfully near the secret.

"Are you sure? It might be better that you use my poor skill tonight. It's important, dear sir, that we make sure you are strong and energized for this special occasion. The people look for great things from you because they're sure—or at least are afraid— that another year may come around and find their pastor gone."

"Yes, to another world," replied the minister with pious resignation. "Heaven grant that it will be a better one for if the truth be told I hardly think to be here with my flock through another year! But your medicine, kind sir, the way I'm presently feeling, I don't need it."

"I rejoice to hear it," answered the physician. "It may be that my remedies are just beginning to take good effect after so long. I'd be a happy man, and well deserving of New England's gratitude, if I could achieve this cure!"

"I thank you from my heart, my watchful friend," said the Reverend Mr. Dimmesdale with a solemn smile. "I thank you and can only repay your good deeds with my prayers."

"A good man's prayers are a golden reward!" said Chillingworth as he took his leave. "Yes, they are the current gold coin of the New Jerusalem with the King's own mint mark on them!"

Left alone, the minister sent for a servant of the house and asked for food and when he got it he ate with a ravenous appetite. Then he flung the already written pages of the Election Sermon into the fire and began over again. He wrote with such an impulsive flow of thought and emotion that he imagined himself inspired and only wondered that Heaven should play its solemn music through so foul an instrument as he was. However, leaving that mystery to solve itself or to go unsolved forever, he pursued his task onward with earnest speed and ecstasy.

The night fled away as if it were a winged horse and he riding it. Morning came and peeped, blushing, through the curtains and at last sunrise threw a golden gleam into the study and laid it right across the minister's bedazzled eyes. There he was, with the pen still between his fingers, and a vast, immeasurable stream of words lying in his wake.

21

The New England Holiday

The new Governor was to receive his office at the hands of the people that morning when Hester Prynne and Pearl came into the marketplace. It was already thronged with the craftsmen and laborers of the town but there were many rough outsiders dressed in deerskins that marked them as belonging to some of the forest settlements.

On days like these Hester was always dressed in a garment of coarse gray cloth. Its color and plainness ensured that she didn't stand out but of course the scarlet letter proclaimed its own message.

Her face had that marble quietness the townspeople were used to; it was like a mask or more like the frozen calmness of a dead woman's features. Socially speaking she was dead and had no claim to sympathy since she had in some sense left the world.

But on this one day, if someone had been especially gifted and had cared one way or another, he might have noticed that there was a look about her that wasn't the same as always. Her habit of walking with her head somewhat bowed so that she wouldn't meet the eyes of people passing was not just as pronounced today. She wasn't striding along in defiance but if you had looked for it you would have seen something of a challenge. It was muted, to be sure, but it had a, "Take your last look on the scarlet letter and the woman that wears it!" suggestion. The people's victim and lifelong bond-slave, as they imagined her, might say to them, "Before too long I will be beyond your reach! A few hours longer and the deep ocean will quench and bury forever the symbol you made to flame on my breast!" Would she miss it? How could she? And yet...people are strange creatures. For years it had so marked her out that it had given her a social identity and shaped not only the way she thought but also the way she carried herself and behaved. It had molded her expectations and her responses and her relationships with people, places, and even objects. Perhaps, then, it isn't an inconsistency too improbable that at the moment when she was about to gain her freedom there would be a feeling of regret in Hester's mind. Don't prisoners feel such things when they come face to face with freedom after so long in prison? The wine of life from now on would be rich, delicious and exhilarating or it would be bland or almost tasteless after the bitter cordial she had been drugged with. And don't criminals feel that also when they're back to the ordinary pace and ways of living? The excitement of the battle is gone, the stubborn defiance that refuses the shackles of social acceptability has no outlet—they feel at a loss.

Pearl had no such questions in her head, decked out with frivolous gaiety. No one could have guessed that this little girl came from this sober woman or that the heart and skill of that same woman had created this bright and sunny apparition and the dull, shapeless gray of her own dress. Pearl and her dress were one—each, it seemed, an extension of the other. She was always capricious, always fidgety and on the move but there was an added edge and shimmer and throbbing in her that day. She picked it up from her mother for perceptive children pick up on such things as long grass picks up on the very slightest breeze. The nervy trembling that Hester suppressed played more openly on the strings of the personality of her daughter who repeatedly broke into wild shouts and sometimes piercing music.

When they reached the market she became still more restless in the restless surroundings. What was normally the broad and lonesome green in front of a village meeting house was now the pulsating center of the town's business. Her words tumbled out in time with the flurry around her.

"What is this, mother? Why have all the people left their work today? Is it a play-day for the whole world? Look, there's the blacksmith all clean and dressed up! He looks like he'd be pleased to be happy if somebody would only teach him how! And there's Master Brackett, the old jailer, nodding and smiling at me. Why does he do that, mother?"

"He remembers you when you were a little baby," Hester said.

Unimpressed she rattled back, "Well, he has no right to nod and smile at me. The grim, ugly-eyed old man! He may nod at you if he wants for you're dressed in gray and wear the scarlet letter. But look how many strange people there are here. Why are they all here?"

"They want to see the procession pass. The Governor and the magistrates are to go by, and the ministers, and all the great and good people. There's going to be music and soldiers marching."

"And will the minister be here?" asked Pearl. "And will he hold out both his hands to me the way he did beside the brook?"

"He'll be there, child," she said, "but he won't greet you to-day and you are not to greet him."

"What a strange sad man he is!" said the child, as if speaking to herself. "In the night he calls us to him and holds your hand and mine, like when we stood with him on the scaffold! And in the deep forest, where only the old trees can hear and the sky can see, he talks with you and kisses my forehead. But, here, in the sunny day and among all the people he doesn't knows us and we're not to know him! A strange, sad man with his hand always over his heart!"

"Be quiet, Pearl—you don't understand these things," said her mother. "Forget the minister and pay attention to how cheerful everybody is today. A new man is to begin to rule over them and they believe he will make the coming year prosperous and golden so they're celebrating. Hester had summarized it correctly. On this inauguration day the Puritans expressed as much joy and pleasure as they thought was allowable to sinful humans. So different was the tone on this single day that they were nearly as cheerful as most other communities are at a period of general affliction.

214

Well, that's something of an exaggeration. They were more cheerful than that since the people now in the Boston market had not inherited puritanical gloom. They were native Englishmen, whose fathers had lived in the sunny richness of the Elizabethan reign, a time when the life of England as a whole would appear to have been as stately, magnificent, and joyous as the world has ever witnessed.

Had they followed their earlier customs the New England settlers would have celebrated public occasions with bonfires, banquets, pageants as well as processions. And why not? For all the solemnity of such occasions they were supposed to be for the good of the people and if that wasn't a reason to celebrate there never was one.

It was important to maintain the dignity of the government and treat the representatives of the people with respect and honor, so the pomp and splendor was appropriate. But the dignity and honor conferred shouldn't be allowed to hide the joy of the people that such honorable men were to lead to golden prosperity. Pomp, splendor and dignity were not enemies of joy and gladness and the expression of such feelings.

But while it was true that the people were encouraged to take a break from their hard toil and be glad, there was a limit set to the kind of entertainment that was permitted. The England of Elizabeth's time would have been more liberal in that respect but in this New England territory fewer forms of entertainment got by the city fathers. There would be no rude shows of a theatrical kind, no minstrel with his harp and legendary ballad, no entertainer with an ape dancing to his music, no juggler with his tricks of mimic

215

witchcraft and no clown to stir up the multitude with antics and gestures. The law and the general sentiment that give law its vitality would have frowned on all that. Still, the great and honest face of the people smiled—grimly perhaps but widely too. And of course there were sports. These were encouraged because they fostered manliness and courage. There were wrestling matches with various rules, depending on whether it was Cornwall or Devonshire wrestling. There were friendly bouts with quarter-staffs and—what attracted most interest of all—on the platform of the pillory two masters of defense were demonstrating with the buckler and broadsword. But the town beadle took a dim view of it being conducted on so sacred a spot and shut the exhibition down.

On the whole the people enjoyed their holidays as well as we do today. It was the generation next to the early emigrants that wore the gloomiest shade of Puritanism and gave it such a horrible face; so horrible that all the years since then have not been enough to wipe it clean. We have yet to learn again the forgotten art of enjoying ourselves and being glad.

A party of Indians—in their savage finery of embroidered deerskin robes, wampum-belts, red and yellow in color, feathers and armed with the bow and arrow and stone-headed spear—they stood apart with faces like stone, even more sober than the Puritan look. But they weren't the wildest looking group on the scene. That distinction could more justly be claimed by part of the crew of the vessel from the Spanish Main that had come ashore to see the events of Election Day. They were rough-looking desperadoes, with sun-blackened faces, great beards, wide short trousers belted at the waist with buckles made of rough plates of gold. They had long knives and in a few cases they had swords. From beneath their broad-brimmed hats of palm-leaf animal eyes gleamed. They cared nothing for rules and regulations that kept people in line. They would smoke tobacco right under the beadle's nose and guzzle draughts of wine or alcohol from pocket flasks, freely offering them to the gaping crowd around them.

Today we would call these sailors pirates and there's not a doubt that if they did today the things they did back then they would have risked their necks in a court of law.

It has always seemed strange to me that they were given such liberty to do on sea what no man would have been allowed to do on land. And if one of these buccaneers decided to quit the sea and cultivate an orchard on land no one would have thought it strange.

Nor would his riotous past mean he was not fit company for the proper citizen on land. That's why the Puritan elders in their black cloaks, starched bands and steeple-crowned hats smiled indulgently at the clamor and rude behavior of these jolly seafaring men. That being the case no one gave it a second thought when someone as reputable as citizen Roger Chillingworth entered the marketplace and had a long and amicable talk with the commander of the wild vessel.

As far as clothing went, the commander was a more showy and gallant figure than anyone else in the teeming crowd. His chest was covered with ribbons and there was gold lace on his hat surrounded by a gold chain and a feather topped it off. He had a sword at his side and a sword-cut on his forehead; by the way he parted his hair he obviously wanted to show it off rather than hide it. Clothes like that would have brought a land-lubber a fine, if he were fortunate, or a day or two in the stocks. On the shipmaster the clothes were seen as naturally a part of him as glistening scales on a fish.

The commander of the Bristol ship strolled idly through the marketplace until he saw and recognized Hester Prynne who stood in a small vacant area—a sort of magic circle—had usually formed around her. It had its own moral message to tell but it worked out well because it allowed Hester and the captain to speak without being overheard. But so changed was Hester Prynne's reputation before the public that no one that noticed would have dreamed there was anything scandalous going on.

"So, mistress," said the sailor, cheerful in tone, "I need to tell the steward to prepare for one more berth than you bargained for! There's no fear of scurvy or ship fever on this voyage. If there's any danger at all it will be from drugs or pills. What with the ship's surgeon and now this other doctor there's a lot of apothecary's stuff aboard."

"What do you mean?" inquired Hester, startled more than she let herself show. "Have you another passenger?"

"You mean you didn't know?" cried the shipmaster, "The physician here—Chillingworth he calls himself—he's to try my cabin-fare with you. Ay, ay, you must have known it for he told me he's one of your party and a close friend to the gentleman you spoke of—the man that's in danger from these sour old Puritan rulers."

"They know each other well, indeed," replied Hester, acting calmly, though agitated beyond measure. "They have long dwelt together."

218

That ended the conversation. But at that instant she saw Roger Chillingworth himself, standing in the remote comer of the marketplace and smiling at her. Even across the wide and bustling square and through all the talk and laughter and various thoughts, moods, and interests of the crowd—the smile was sinister and threatening.

22

The Procession

Hester's mind was reeling. What was to be done? How did Chillingworth get to know their plans? How could she tell Arthur without his falling apart? She couldn't think straight and to make matters worse suddenly a military band struck up and was heading her way with instruments clashing and sounding. The mass procession of magistrates with the high ranking and ordinary citizens following was on its way toward the meeting-house where the Reverend Mr. Dimmesdale would deliver the Election Sermon to an adoring congregation.

Here came the procession headed by the marching band that raised the emotions and made people believe they were really part of a heroic movement of history. Trumpets, drums and cymbals filled the air while children danced and old people stamped and remembered.

Pearl laughed, clapped but then was mesmerized by the military men that followed, armor gleaming and weapons at the ready. They were the guard of honor escorting the high ranking and didn't they look impressive with the sun shimmering and shining on them! Stirring tunes, piercing trumpets, thunderous drums and brave soldiers in burnished steel blazing and blinding in the sunlight with plumage nodding, marching shoulder to shoulder in a display of visible unity and power. It made a person feel great to be alive and to be part of such a vibrant New England colony! Behind them came the men that truly kept the colony together. If the music and the troops stirred the emotions these respected men stirred something deeper. The very appearance of the white-haired, wise and dependable men spoke of stability and experience. They hadn't come to stay a day but had sowed their entire lives in the field of the people and with that faithful commitment there came a depth of understanding that gave strength to the muscles and sinews of the wilderness community. These early statesmen therefore— Bradstreet, Endicott, Dudley, Bellingham, and their like—who were elevated to power by the choice of the people were not esteemed for their brilliance but distinguished by a ponderous steadiness. They had courage and self-reliance and in time of difficulty or danger they stood up for the welfare of the state like a line of cliffs against the shock of thunderous waves that would have overwhelmed the land.

Then came the man of the hour, the young and highly distinguished divine who would deliver the religious discourse. But this was a new Dimmesdale. There was no sign of the feebleness and beaten way of walking they had come to know and expect! None at all! He looked brimful of energy and eagerness as he marched the street to his place and there was no hand over the heart! But this wasn't physical strength—it was more than that and the roots went deeper than his sinews and muscles. And how had this happened? Where did he get this newly found energy and excitement? Nobody knew, and while they might have wondered they didn't really care because they were too happy to see him as he was, forget the analysis that could come later. He was so much in the grip of powerful truth that the mind was feeding the body and the nerves.

But while he marched they looked at his eyes and wondered where his mind was! Like an eagle that has spotted its prey a long way off and sees nothing else in the entire world as its flies, so the minister was lost in a vision. He was lost in his message and so captured by the majesty of what filled his mind he saw nothing, heard nothing and knew nothing of what was going on around him. He might not have an ounce of strength in his body when he was done but until that time he was committing all the resources within him.

The spirit had grabbed the feeble frame and made it capable of one mighty exhibition of power and concentration.

Hester Prynne stared at him and all of a sudden she was frightened, thinking she had lost him. But surely their eyes would meet and they would sense the union and think again of a little dell and a moss covered pine tree. But was this the man? She hardly knew him now. Look at him marching proudly past, wrapped in the rich music, respected by the venerable fathers and guarded to the death by the troops. He was on the crest of an enormous wave and she was the last thing in his mind. She felt her world collapsing and he didn't care. He had found his place and no longer felt the need of her; her old bitterness returned with her growing feeling of rejection.

Pearl saw him too and in only a moment she confirmed Hester's worst fears.

"Was that the same minister that kissed me by the brook?" Hester had no time for more of Pearl's strange insights.

"Be quiet Pearl! What happened to us in the forest is not to be discussed here."

"I couldn't be sure that it was him, he looked so different," said the aggravating child. "If I'd been sure I might have run to him and asked him kiss me now in front of all the people. What would the minister have said, do you think? Would he have clapped his hand over his heart and told me to go away?"

"It was well for you that thou didn't speak to him, you silly child!" As if that weren't enough Mistress Hibbins walked over, dressed to the heavens and as mad as ever. Before too long they would hang her for promoting witchcraft and devilry but in the meantime she flaunted it and had the protection of her relationship with the magistrate Bellingham. As Hibbins approached the superstitious crowd moved away and left the two noted figures to themselves.

"Now, who'd have thought it?" she whispered to Hester. "Look at him. He looks every inch what the people think he is but you and I know better, don't we? He might chew Hebrew scriptures in his mouth but he makes visits to the forest, doesn't he. But I find it hard to believe he's the same man. I saw a lot of church members in that procession walking behind the music on their way to church—they were the same people that danced with me in the forest when you know who was the fiddler. But that's a sheer trifle when a woman knows the world. This is different. Can you assure me that that minister is the same man that met you on the forest path?"

"Madam, I don't know what you're talking about," snapped Hester, jolted to learn that so many people were involved with the Evil One. "And it isn't for me to speak lightly of a learned and pious minister of the Word, like the Reverend Dimmesdale."

"You're a liar!" cried the old lady shaking her finger at Hester. "Do thou think I don't know these things? There may be no leaves or grass on them when they come back from the forest but I know those that go there and I know you, Hester Prynne. But at least your sign is out in the open, shining by day and flaming by night but this minister," she spat out the words. "Let me tell you, when the Dark One sees one of his own signed and sealed servants so ashamed of admitting the bond as the Reverend Mr. Dimmesdale is, he has a way of bringing it out into the daylight so that everyone can see. What do you think it is that he keeps covering up with his hand over his heart, huh?"

Pearl as usual had something to say. "What is it, Mistress Hibbins, have you seen it?"

"It doesn't matter, darling!" Hibbins said, bowing to Pearl as if in profound reverence. "You'll see it yourself sooner or later. You know, people say you are of the lineage of the Prince of Air! Would you like to ride with me some night to see your father? You'd find out then why the minister keeps his hand over his heart!" She walked away laughing so shrilly that half the marketplace could hear her.

By this time the Reverend Mr. Dimmesdale had begun his message. Hester couldn't leave; she couldn't get into the building either because it was packed to the roof so she stayed close to the scaffold of the pillory. Walls or no walls, she was close enough to hear what Arthur was saying. She didn't understand the big words but she understood enough profound truth to be moved and enlightened and inspired by it. But it wasn't only what he said it was how he said it. Everything about his voice, his highs and lows, his whisper and his thunder—all of it served the message that simply demanded to be heard. This was no original thinker that was making it up as he went, giving his opinion on this and that—it was all beyond control. He was a voice being used by a word from heaven. No, more than a voice, but a voice! And with the voice came a heart and through that heart with all its experiences the Word made itself known. The wind of Heaven was blowing through the town and the colony and the world...and single human hearts.

In and through it all there was the sigh of human unhappiness, of suffering mankind. The minister's plaintive sighs and desolate silences became theirs. Emotion filled the very air; emotion made electric by the truth that created it until it seemed it would break down the church walls and echo through the whole blessed earth. How do you explain it when such events take place? Is it the lament of a human heart, sorrow-laden, maybe guilty, in its own way telling its secret, whether of guilt or sorrow to the great heart of mankind, at every moment and in each tone begging its sympathy or forgiveness and never asking in vain? Perhaps it was here that the minister and his word had its vast power. Perhaps it was here that the Word and its minister had its profound power.

She stood like a statue at the foot of the scaffold--riveted. Even if the minister's voice hadn't kept her there it was the magnetism of that spot. Though too vague to be a conscious thought she felt that this place made sense of all her life before and after.

Pearl was doing what Pearl always did—what pleased her! She danced her way around the market until she caught the attention of the ship's captain who wanted to kiss her. He would have if he could have caught her but there was little chance of that—she was too quick. He threw his golden chain to her and she promptly wound it round her.

"Will you give your mother a message from me?" he asked.

"If I like the message I will," she rattled back.

"Then tell her that I spoke again with hump shouldered old doctor and he said he would see to it that that gentleman we talked about gets on board with him. So your mother will only have herself and you to take care of. Will you tell her that you little witch?"

"Mistress Hibbins says my father is the Prince of the Air!" she shouted contemptuously. "If you call me that again I'll tell him about you and he'll chase your ship with a storm!" She found her mother and told her. Hester's spirit sank. For a while it had looked as if freedom was possible but the old man, crippled in body and more twisted in mind and heart was going to see to it that they'd be prisoners forever.

She hadn't realized it but she had become the center of attraction.

There was a host of strangers in town that had heard stories about the woman with the scarlet letter and now that they knew she was in the market they wanted to get a look at her. It's no surprise that many of the stories were fictitious or exaggerated but what difference does that make to curious people? The wilder the stories the greater the curiosity. And if it happened that one or two stories were true then all the rest are believed on the basis of the truth of a few. Anyway, there was nothing else to amuse them since they'd seen everything so why not gawk at Hester for a while; and there they were elbowing one another to get a good view. Imagine her in the center of a huge crowd of jostling people, separated from them by a yard or so—a freak show. A whole gang of sailors, having learned what the scarlet letter meant thought they'd like to see the woman; who knows, she might be available to them.

What a turn around! Just when she was sure that she would soon be done with the scarlet letter and that it would never again draw a crowd, it had attracted a whole new generation of viewers. How many sinners are there, do you suppose, that thought they were done with some shameful past only to find the old story resurrected and their healed wounds ripped wide open again? While Hester stood in that circle where the cunning cruelty of her sentence seemed to have fixed her for ever, the honored preacher was looking down from the sacred pulpit on a congregation that had given him control over their very souls. The sainted minister in the church! The fallen woman in the marketplace! Who—inside the building or out of it— in their wildest dreams could have imagined that the same scorching stigma was on them both?

23

The Revelation of the Scarlet Letter

The Election Sermon ended. There was a momentary silence; the kind you might expect following profound words from an oracle. Then murmuring began as the spellbound came back from the other world where he had taken them; but they brought back with them all their awe and wonder. A quiet pandemonium developed and the pressure mounted until they could stay no longer. The building disgorged the smitten worshipers out through the doors and on to the street where, free from the muting confines of the sanctuary, they could breathe and trumpet their rapturous astonishment. The entire town-square rang with unbridled praise for the minister. They couldn't keep quiet until they had told one another what each knew and knew better than he could tell or hear.

The huge crowd agreed on this: nobody had ever spoken like that! Never had inspiration breathed through mortal lips more unmistakably than it did through his. Why, it was more than feeling, more than hearing—you could almost see it! Notes? Well, maybe he looked at them now and then but he had risen far beyond what he had studied and written on the paper. Thoughts were being freshly delivered to him as he stood there, and everybody sensed it; thoughts that must have been as profound and marvelous to him as they were to them.

Only someone blind and deaf and without a heart to feel could have missed it. What had happened inside that building had never happened anywhere else in the country and the like of it would never happen again. The great grandchildren of those who were there this day would still be telling about it in awe-smitten tones to their grandchildren.

And as he had drawn to a close a spirit as of prophecy had come on him, compelling him as mightily as it had done the prophets of Israel; a compulsion to proclaim blessing and not judgement. It had been given to him to foretell a high and glorious destiny for the newly gathered people of the Lord in the New England they were attempting to build here in this wild and heathen land.

All that wondrous enough, thrilling enough, but in the warp and woof of it there was a throb, a sad undertone. He proclaimed with power and assurance that he had a dream but everyone sensed that he wouldn't be there to see it with them. He spoke no word about himself and yet they many felt they were seeing and hearing him for the last time. They didn't know how to take it other than as the minister's realization that he would soon die. Yes, their minister, the one they so loved and who so loved them was leaving them with hope in their hearts for the future and tears in their eyes for their coming loss. In their hearts they had always known it, he was an angel of light, Heaven had given him to them only for a little while and now it was time for him to return.

He stood at this moment on the pinnacle of perfection to which the gifts of intellect, eloquence and a reputation of whitest sanctity could exalt a clergyman in New England's earliest days. That's where he was as he bowed his head forward on the cushions of the pulpit at the close of his Election Sermon. Meanwhile—Hester stood beside the scaffold of the pillory.

The music began, the procession was gathering to march to the town hall for the banquet that would end the proceedings. The crowd moved back while the leaders formed themselves and then with one voice the huge throng recognized the leaders with a thunderous shout—a tidal wave pounding against immovable and massive cliffs.

But while it was true that they had shouted for the faithful magistrates and their civic supporters, there was no doubt who was at the center of their thoughts. Never on the soil of New England had a man so spoken. Never from the soil of New England had gone up such a shout! Never on New England soil stood a man so honored by his mortal brethren as this preacher! And how did he take it all? Every eye turned toward the point where the minister would become visible. The buzz and the noise died into a murmur as one portion of the crowd after another caught sight of him. Sick and feeble and ghostly. The inspiration that had held him up long enough for him to deliver the sacred message was gone—he was empty now. The glow they'd seen burning on his cheek like a flame was gone—he was ashes now. He wasn't alive; they saw a dead man walking. He tottered as he moved, tottered without falling.

John Wilson hurriedly stepped forward to offer his support but the minister wouldn't have it. He staggered with the uncertain but determined effort of an infant with a goal in view, until he came opposite the weather-beaten scaffold. There stood Hester with the little girl by the hand—scarlet letter and all! There he stopped. The band played on but he stopped.

Bellingham had kept an anxious eye on him for the last few moments and now moved to assist him because he looked as if he were going to fall. But there was something in Dimmesdale's expression that warned him to leave it be. The crowd was mesmerized. They didn't know what to expect but it wouldn't have surprised many of them if he ascended into heaven right in front of their eyes! But he didn't turn toward heaven; he turned toward the scaffold and the woman and he stretched out his arms.

"Hester," he said, "come here! Come here my little Pearl!" There was something ghastly about it, a look of triumph mingled with tenderness. The child flew to him and wrapped her arms around his knees. Hester moved toward him, slowly, as if she really didn't want to but she stopped before she reached him. At this very moment misshapen Roger Chillingworth—the minister's doctor they said, the minister's torturer we say—pushed his way through the crowd; he looked so disturbed and so insanely wicked and he came not to bless but to keep his victim from what he was about to do! He caught the minister by the arm.

232

"You're mad! What are you doing?" he hissed. "Wave the woman away and chase the child! It's not too late. You fool, don't blacken your name and die in dishonor! I can still save you! Do you realize how many people are depending on you and look up to you? Do you mean to injure them and breed cynicism? Do you want to bring infamy on your sacred profession?"

"Aaaah," it was almost a hushed sigh, like the long last breath of a dying man, calm and drawn out. "You're too late Chillingworth!" breathed the minister, for the first time looking him steadily in the eye.

"Your power isn't what it was! With God's help, I triumph over you now!" But he feared to trust himself any longer and cried to the woman to help him.

"Hester Prynne," he shouted with a piercing earnestness, "in the name of God who is so terrible and so merciful and who gives me grace at this last moment, come to me. Let me do what I should have done seven years ago. Help me to do what in sinful cowardice I refused to do because I wanted to protect myself from shame and misery. Come here please and strengthen me. It was your strength used by God that brought me this far; help me finish it! This wretched old man that I wronged so deeply is trying to stop me. His work is Satan's work. Come, Hester, come and help me up these steps to the scaffold."

The crowd was in an uproar. The leaders were stupefied. How could they believe what was going on in front of them? They watched as the minister, leaning on Hester's shoulder and supported by her arm around his waist began to climb the steps up to the scaffold.

Like a ghoul Chillingworth followed and snarled in the minister's ear, "If you had looked the whole earth over to find a place to hide you wouldn't have found one. There is no place deep enough or far enough or secret enough. I would have found you!" The venom oozed from him but so did his frustration and inexpressible rage that his victim was now nearly out of his control. "You couldn't have escaped from me anywhere else in all the world but on this scaffold."

"Then thank God who led me here! Free at last," said the minister. He turned to Hester with a feeble smile on his lips.

"Now isn't this better than what we dreamed of in the forest?"

"I don't know!" she moaned. "Better? Yes, perhaps, and it might be that we will die with you."

"I don't know what God's will is for you and Pearl but God is merciful. I'm about to die Hester and I believe there is one more thing God wants me to do. Help me please. I must make my shame fully known."

She helped support him and holding the child's hand he turned to the stunned crowd. Partly supported by Hester and holding on to Pearl's hand, he turned to the rulers, the holy ministers who were his colleagues and to the people whose great heart was thoroughly appalled yet overflowing with tearful sympathy. They knew that a life and death matter was being revealed to them and if it was full of sin it was also full of anguish and repentance. It was just past noon, when he stood to make his plea of guilty at the bar of Eternal Justice.

"People of New England! You that have loved me, you that have judged me to be holy—look at me now, the chief sinner of the world!

At last—at last I stand on the spot where I should have stood seven years ago with this woman who keeps me on my feet at this dreadful moment. Without her I would be groveling on the earth at your feet! You can see the scarlet letter she wears! You've all shuddered at it! Everywhere she went it brought her stares and scorn but there was one among you whose brand of sin and infamy didn't make you shudder." He was obviously working up to something but it was also clear that it wasn't easy and that he was on the edge of collapse. All of a sudden he stepped in front of the woman and cried with a loud voice.

"You didn't shudder at it because you didn't see it. But the brand was on him! God's eye saw it! The angels were always pointing at it! The Devil knew it well and constantly picked at it with the touch of his burning finger! But he sinner cunningly hid it from men and walked among you with a mournful spirit as though he was a pure man in a world of sinners. But he was lonely because he had no fellowship because he knew he wasn't worthy of it! I'm that sinner! Now I'm about to die. I want you to look again at Hester's scarlet letter! With all its mysterious horror it's only a shadow of what I carry on my chest, my own red stigma and that is only a pale image of what is burned on my heart. Is there any among you that doubts whether God brings judgment on sinners? Then look, see the proof! He ripped open his shirt and there it was. It would be wrong to describe what he revealed. The crowd had been deeply moved and now they were horror-stricken as they stared at the ghastly thing. The minister stood swaying with a flush of triumph on his face—he had won a victory. He collapsed; Hester sat down beside him, took him in her arms and held him against her breast. Chillingworth knelt down beside him with a blank, dull look. His life drained out of him, he had no more purpose.

"You've escaped me!" he repeated more than once. "You've escaped me!"

"May God forgive you!" said the minister. "You've sinned deeply also!" He was done with the old man and fixed his dying eyes on the woman and the child.

"My Pearl," he whispered. "now will you kiss me?" Pearl kissed his lips. A spell was broken and a spring deep inside her rushed to the surface. The child began to sob and left her tears on her father's face. The wild child died that day too and her tears were the pledge of it. She brought no more anguish to her mother; those days were done.

"Goodbye Hester," he said.

"We'll meet again, won't we?" she said, leaning close. "We'll share eternal life together, won't we? Surely...surely with all this woe the torment is ended! Look with those bright eyes of yours and tell me what you see for us."

"Hush, Hester, hush! The law we broke...the awful sin revealed here..." words of consolation and assurance wouldn't come, "we must keep this in mind. I'm afraid, so afraid. Maybe because we forgot our God, because we violated our reverence for each other's soul that there's no possibility that we can meet in peace and joy. God knows and he is merciful! He has proved his mercy to me in my afflictions.

"By giving me this burning torture to bear upon my chest! By sending that terrible old man and by bringing me here to die this death of triumphant shame before the people! Without these

236

agonies I know I would have been lost forever. Praised be his name! His will be done!"

With his last breath he whispered, "Goodbye!" The silent host broke out in a deep wordless groan of awe, wonder and grief.

24

Conclusion

What happened at the scaffold? What did the people see? Obviously there were things everyone could agree on but on a number of crucial things people held decidedly different views.

Most of the spectators swore that when the dying minister tore open his shirt they saw a scarlet letter—the perfect image of the one worn by Hester Prynne. It was burned into his flesh. How it got there was another question and anyone's guess. There were those that insisted that on the very day that Hester Prynne first wore hers that the Reverend Dimmesdale inflicted a hideous wound on himself. Others contended that the stigma hadn't appeared until much later; in fact, they said, it only appeared when old Roger Chillingworth, a powerful necromancer, made it appear with the use of magic and poisonous drugs. Others, who understand how closely the body is tied to the mind in very sensitive people, whispered their belief that the awful symbol was the effect of the remorse that gnawed its way out from his heart. The reader may choose among these theories. I have thrown all the light on the sign that I could get and I would gladly put it completely out of my mind.

But here is a strange thing. Certain people, who were spectators of the whole scene and swore that they never once took their eyes off the Reverend Dimmesdale, denied that there was any mark of any kind on his chest! These same people insist that the minister never said or even implied that he was connected with Hester Prynne's sin. According to these highly respected witnesses the minister wanted to cure the multitude of their sin of exalting him beyond his station. He arranged it so that he would die in the arms of a fallen woman to express to the world the utter vanity of any man's own righteousness. He arranged the way he died to teach his admirers a profound truth—that we are all miserable sinners and that human merit is a phantom. I've no wish to dispute a truth so important but I consider this version of Mr. Dimmesdale's story as an instance of that stubborn refusal of friends to admit the sin of their friends. I think it's especially true of a clergyman's friends. They'll dispute clear proofs that establish him to be a false and sin-stained creature of the dust.

The authority we have chiefly followed fully confirms the view taken in the narrative I've recorded. The authority is an aged manuscript drawn up from the verbal testimony of individuals some of whom had known Hester Prynne. There are others that heard the tale from contemporary witnesses.

The experience of the Reverend Dimmesdale teaches us many lessons but I lay out only this: Be true! Be true! Be true! Indicate freely to the world your sinfulness. If you do not reveal your worst at least reveal something from which the worst can be inferred. Make no confessions that function only to hide the truth.

Chillingworth died within a year of Arthur Dimmesdale. Nothing was more remarkable than the way he spiraled downward in appearance and attitude. All his strength and energy, all his vital and intellectual force seemed to leak from him, like water from a cracked cup. He simply withered and died like an uprooted weed that lies wilting in the sun.

Revenge was the driving force of his life and when his victim was gone there was no more Devil's work on earth for him to do and no doubt he went where his master would pay him his wages.

But to all these shadowy beings I would like to be merciful. Love and hate share many things in common (regret at the loss of the object of attention, the need for intimacy and close knowledge of the other). There is a fundamental difference, of course—one shines with heavenly glory and the other with a lurid burning.

The old physician and the minister were mutual victims and in that other realm who knows how the story finally ends.

Governor Bellingham and the Reverend Wilson were executors of Roger Chillingworth's will and in it he bequeathed a very considerable amount of property, both here and in England to Pearl.

So Pearl, the demon offspring as some people considered her became the richest woman of her day in the New World. One thing is certain, that would have changed the way Pearl was viewed and if she had remained here she might have mingled her wild blood with the most devout Puritans of them all. But not long after the doctor died mother and daughter disappeared. Now and then rumors would make their way to this region but that's all they remained—rumors. The story of the scarlet letter grew into a legend and gave the scaffold where the poor minister had died and the cottage by the seashore where Hester Prynne had dwelt a lasting mystique and awfulness. One afternoon some children were playing near the cottage when they saw a tall woman in gray go to the cottage door. The house has been deserted all those years but she unlocked it or the decaying wood and iron crumbled or she walked through them. Whatever—she did go in.

On the threshold she hesitated, almost completely turned away but then chose to enter. But as she turned they saw a scarlet letter on her breast.

Hester Prynne had returned! But where was Pearl? If still alive, by then she must have been in the bloom of early womanhood. Nobody knew what had happened. Did she die young, unmarried? Did she soften into a gentle woman and enjoy happiness? No one knows but someone from another land sent important looking letters and expensive gifts to Hester throughout the rest of her life. And once Hester was seen embroidering a baby garment that wasn't suited for any baby of the lower social levels.

The gossips of that day believed—and Mr. Pue, who investigated it all a century later, believed—that Pearl was not only alive, but married and was happy and mindful of her mother and wished her to live with her.

But there was more real life for Hester Prynne here in New England. Here she had sinned, here she had experienced her sorrow, here she had loved and here she would live out her penitence. She took up again the insignia that carried no more stigma and became a type of something to be sorrowed over. People brought all their sorrows and perplexities and asked her counsel as one who had been through a mighty trouble.

########

Thank you for reading and I trust, enjoying this book. If you have any inquiries or questions feel free to write to me.

Jim McGuiggan

holywoodjk@aol.com

www.jimmcguiggan.com/